PRAISE FOR STEPHEN MERTZ

"One of my favorite writers ... a born storyteller ... Enjoy!"

--Max Allan Collins, NYT Bestselling author of *Road to Perdition* and the *Quarry* series.

"One of the best adventure writers of our time!"

--NYT Bestselling writer James Reasoner

"Stephen Mertz just keeps on getting better, each novel more dazzling in story and style!"

--Ed Gorman

THE VAMPIRE CHASE

THE STEVE MADISON MYSTERIES

STEPHEN MERTZ

WOLFPACK
PUBLISHING
— EST 2013 —

The Vampire Chase
The Steve Madison Mysteries
Stephen Mertz

Paperback Edition
Copyright © 2018 (as revised) Stephen Mertz

Wolfpack Publishing
6032 Wheat Penny Ave
Las Vegas, NV 89122

Paperback ISBN 978-1-64119-539-3
eBook ISBN 978-1-64119-538-6

Library of Congress Control Number: 2018963807

For Eagle Park Slim

THE VAMPIRE CHASE

THE POWER WAS WITH HIM, STRONGER THAN EVER NOW.

It raced through his body, sending him higher than any drug ever could. It was always this way after a concert. The piercing, multi-colored stage lights. The hammering, high-powered waves of sound from the banks of amplifiers. The screams from out front. They seemed to ignite the raw energy humming through his veins, pulsating, screaming - out for release.

And the release had to be sexual.

But then there was the other need. It too had been building. It didn't come as often as the sexual craving, but it was always near, waiting to take possession of his very soul. Waiting to answer the call. The call had come to him this time, as always, onstage. The strongest of a kaleidoscope of sensations swirling around and through him amid the pounding, well-trembling assault of Rock in full fury.

It was Lucifer's call to do Lucifer's bidding, and he

had learned long ago how useless it was to ignore the call or to fight it. There was only one recourse. To obey. The need must be fed; satisfied.

With blood.

The girl with him now was perfect.

Perfect for both needs...

She was a groupie. One of those wasted young ladies—this one barely out of her teens—whose world is the motel bedroom and the backstage area of rock concert halls. She had passed inspection on all counts. Height, about five-eight. Breasts, small with a natural upward tilt. Long, flowing blonde hair framing a fairly pretty, stoned, slightly stupid face. All packaged in pure rock world tack. Plenty of makeup, plenty of feathers and beads, and clinging, gaudily hip clothes that advertised everything she had.

They'd met only an hour before at the backstage party following The Screaming Tree's Tuesday night concert. It had been the last gig of a two-day, three-concert booking, and when they filed offstage he'd been more than ready to get loose.

The party had been one of those spaced-out, almost surreal affairs. People. Questions. Noise. Movement. With all of them—the promoters, the media reps, the record company affiliates, the groupies and the hangers-on—dying to meet the stars. And all the stars knew was that another show was wrapped up. It was time to get crazy for a while, to let off steam before catching the jet to the next city on the tour. It was no secret in the industry that if you wanted a booking completed as contracted, you held off the parties until The Tree had finished their last show. Then, anything went. But before that you ran the very real risk of having three dudes too blown out to play that last show. It had happened more than once.

So, he'd met the chick at this post-show party where the dope and booze had flowed as freely as ever. Getting lined up with her had been no problem. That's what she was there for.

She came on with the standard rap about how she loved the group, how she had all their albums, how she was enjoying the party. It had taken ten minutes for her to get around to mentioning that she had a place not far away where they could be alone with a waterbed and plenty of dynamite smoke if he cared to leave the party.

They went to her apartment and blew their heads out completely with some Vietnamese weed which, she said one of The Loose Goose Band members had laid on her. Then they proceeded to make incredible love.

Sex was purely physical, animalistic thing for him tonight. It was the only way it could be, once Lucifer had spoken. The one time he'd *thought* about a girl while they were making love, before he killed her, it had stayed with him, haunted him, for weeks. So, no, he did not think of this one—Lois, she said her name was—as they screwed. He did not think of how close she was to dying.

She had excused herself and he was alone now on the waterbed, smoking another joint. Soft, old-time blues drifted from the cheap speakers of her stereo. They'd balled to the whirling, pumping rhythms of Disco, but the record had run out and she'd placed this one on the turntable on her way' from the room. He gave the impression of total exhaustion, but he hardly heard the music..

She returned to the bedroom, smiling. Nude and natural, without the wild clothes, she seemed almost like a blonde child.

The idea only excited him further.

She knelt on the waterbed and it swayed beneath them. He offered her the joint. She drew a hit and offered it back, but he shook his head. She extinguished the joint in a nearby ashtray and regarded him warmly.

"That was some far out loving." Her voice matched her looks. "Whatcha thinking about?"

"Just tired. Worn out."

"Was it good, baby?"

"It was good," he said, his voice sounding small in the dimness. "Please, hold me."[v]

"The waterbed moved some more as she made herself comfortable. She slid an arm beneath his neck, drawing him to her. There was the natural, musky scent to her of a woman after loving. That was why he waited. He loved the way they smelled then. The scent was usually the last thing he remembered...

She was mothering him, his head in the crook of her arm. The candle beyond her flickered, its light casting the pulsation of her jugular vein in a warm glow. She curled her fingers idly through the strands of his hair as the old black man on the stereo moaned his woes.

"Do you like blues?" she asked lazily.

He didn't respond. The time had come. He drew his face closer to her neck. His chin rubbed across one of her breasts and the nipple grew erect. She purred as she felt his warm breath travel across her throat. He turned onto his side. She could suddenly feel his new, mighty erection pushing against her. She giggled.

"Well," was the last conscious thing she ever said, "I guess we don't want to talk about music, do we?"

The last thing she ever heard was the snarling groan he emitted an instant before he killed her. A groan from the pits of Hell.

His relaxed body became electrified, galvanized, as Hell's lid lifted, and he became one with the awesome, primal force that exploded from the depths of his mind to the surface of reality. His heart slammed against his ribcage with a maniacal beat that no drum solo could ever hope to match.

For you, Lucifer—blood—the blood of living, breathing flesh—offered to you by your servant—to you, Master of Darkness—to you!!!

His mouth closed over her jugular. His teeth snapped. The girl's body arched violently, yanked taut. Nails raked his back spasmodically. The exciting pain washed over him. She gasped once, her lips curling back over teeth in a rictus of surprise and horrible agony. Wide eyes screamed silently, already glazing in the light of the candle.

The blood burst from her like a geyser. He drew back until the pressure subsided.

Presently, he rose and used her shower. Then he dressed, not looking at what was left of her, sprawled across the still rising and falling waterbed. He was already in the process of easing what had happened from his mind. It was never difficult, as he'd been surprised to learn after the first few.

No one saw him leave either the apartment or the building. He walked ten blocks like a man out for a stroll, then hailed a cab. Twenty minutes later he was back at the party. The backstage area of the concert hall was still jammed with drunk, stoned, loose, laughing wild people.

If anyone had missed him, they didn't say so.

2

"STEVE, ARN WILL SEE YOU NOW."

Steve Madison turned from gazing out the thirty-fifth story window above Manhattan. He was a well-structured, five-foot-ten. His hair, worn too long for New York, the drooping moustache and the western denim—all proclaimed that here was an out-of-towner. Yet there was about him the easy confidence, the quiet strength beneath the surface of nonchalance and the smooth grace of movement of a man who is at home anywhere.

"Thanks, Connie," he said to the receptionist.

He stepped past her desk and entered Arn Shapiro's private office.

Shapiro was second-generation music business and proud of it. His father and an uncle had migrated with their families from the slums of Poland to the slums of America as an alternative to Hitler's ovens. They'd originally gone into the tavern business, had done well, and this had somehow led to the recording and marketing of records by the artists who performed in their club. The marketing had been local at first, but in 1955 a black Rhythm & Blues singer gave the Shapiro Brothers' Jump-Town label its first national hit, and many more had followed. Irv and Stan Shapiro were gone now. In fact, the family no longer had any ties at all with JumpTown although, as the subsidy of a large oil corporation, it was still a thriving concern catering to the jazz audience.

But the music business was still in the Shapiro blood. Or "the game," as Arn liked to call it. After Bill Graham, Arn Shapiro at thirty-seven was the most powerful booking agent/promoter in the world of rock today.

He rose from behind his broad desk and came around to greet Madison, his right arm outstretched He was a meaty, but in-shape guy, his hair a hard, wiry black, a bit on the eccentric, windblown side, with barely noticeable traces of silver running here and there. He was dressed in a natty black pinstripe.

His handshake and manner were cordial yet firm.

"Steve, good to see you. Have a seat. Care for a drink first?"'

His left arm circled Madison's shoulder. Madison allowed himself to be led to a chair.

"No thanks, Arn. Too early. I just flew in."

"Not too early for a smoke. Or some coke."

He wasn't talking about tobacco. Or soft drinks. "Too early for me," Madison said. He took the seat and watched Shapiro return to his desk. "It was a long flight, Arn. You said it was something that couldn't wait."

Shapiro cleared his throat. There was a folded newspaper laying on his desk. He nudged it forward.

"I want you to read something. Page seven, third column, halfway down."

He sat back and waited. Madison took the paper. It was yesterday's *Cleveland Plain Dealer*. He thumbed through it to the specified article. Crime news must have been played down in Cleveland. The inherent sensationalism of the story was disguised beneath the simple heading: *Girl's Body Found* He read the story through twice. There wasn't much to it, wordage-wise. No more than a few paragraphs. A young woman had been found dead by her friends in her walkup apartment, about ten- thirty that morning. The girl's name was Lois Bandy. It was a vicious murder. Her throat had been ripped apart. The body had been nude, stretched across her waterbed, and there were no signs of a struggle. It was a sex crime.

Madison refolded the paper, placed it back on the desk.

"You do it, Arn?"

Shapiro made a face.

"We got trouble, dammit, and I didn't call you all the way back here from your damn mountains to go wiseass on me."

"Let's hear it."

Shapiro emitted a long, tired sigh. "What do you know about The Screaming Trees?" he asked.

"What I read in *Rolling Stone* and the trades. They out kink The Sex Pistols and Alice Cooper on record and outdraw them in concert too. They're the one big act you haven't been able to book on the tube and there are even some cities that won't touch them. They're into an occult trip. Black magic, devil worship, all that crap. They've got one of the raunchiest stage-shows around. Mick Adamson, the lead singer, has been arrested twice for indecent exposure during performance. And the kids love it. It's rebellion, 1978-style. Announce a tour and you're guaranteed of every gig being sold out before the tour begins. Enough?"'

"Enough except for. the biggie. But I can't blame you for missing that. I just put it together myself five minutes before I called you last night. About ten minutes before I had the worst ulcer attack in my whole, goddamn life!"

"I didn't think you sounded your usual cheery self," Madison said dryly. "But I figured it was just the connection. So okay, Arn. You snapped your fingers and here I am. What've you got?"

Shapiro rose and moved to the tall window behind his desk, gazing out and down like a man contemplating a quick exit from everything, including his millions.

"I'm just guessing," he said, not turning. "I maybe way off beam. It may just be crazy coincidence. But I don't think so."_

Madison nodded to the newspaper. "You think one of the boys in the Tree had something to do with that?"

"It doesn't add up any other way."

"You haven't been into hallucinogenic lately, have you, Arn?'"

Shapiro returned to his chair. Madison couldn't remember ever seeing him this uptight before.

"I generally book the Tree on three tours per year. That might sound like a lot when people like the Stones or Dylan are doing one in three but hell. When you're hot, you're hot. Those boys are riding a gimmick. All that occult shit. But people are still interested in it. When they start losing that interest The Screaming Tree is dead. So, I keep them busy. They're working an American tour now. And the night before last they played Cleveland."

"There's got to be more to it than that."

"There is." Just thinking about it seemed to make Shapiro's face twitch. He touched his abdomen. "Jeez, these ulcers!"

"What makes you think the Tree's involved with that girl's death, Arn?"

Shapiro sighed.

"Because it's happened before," he said. "But seldom enough and far apart enough, that no one's made the connection." He slapped an open palm down on the desktop. The sound of flesh on wood echoed in the spacious office. "But *I've* made the connection, dammit, and I want something done about it!"

"You pay me to get things done," Madison said. "But

I must be a little slow on the uptake this morning. You're saying that what happened the other night in Cleveland has happened before on Screaming Tree tours? That girls have been wasted like that when the Tree was in their town?"

"That's exactly what I'm saying. It doesn't look so good, does it?"

"How many times has it happened?"

"The girl in Cleveland was the fourth. I started getting ideas after number three but...hell, you know how it is."

"Yeah. It's a million-dollar act."

Shapiro didn't miss the sarcasm.

"It's also a wild ass crazy idea that could be full of shit," he snarled.

"Don't try to talk yourself out of it this late in the game," said Madison. "You already paid my air fare back here. So, you think one of the boys in the band has a taste for blood, is that it?" His mouth tightened in distaste. "Count Dracula, meet rock 'n roll."

"I get the papers of any city in any country where one of my acts is playing," said Shapiro. "It's probably the only way anyone could make the connection. The first time was in Amsterdam about a year-and- a-half ago. Six months later it happened again L.A. Three months after that I booked them on a British tour with Fleetwood Mac and it happened again, in Manchester. Now, Cleveland. And it's always the same. A hippie, a groupie chick, a nobody. Dead with their throat open from ear to ear."

Madison's eyes were cold.

"Everybody's a somebody, Arn. It sounds like one of your boys deserves to have his head blown off."

Shapiro raised a hand.

"Now don't start talking like that again," he said: "The only reason you got away with it in Nashville was because those bastards you blew away were pushers and the cops couldn't do a thing to bust them anyway. They were glad to see the job get done."

"And you were glad when that singer of yours finally went up for the cure and RCA would talk to him again. What was the figure on that deal, Arn? About a quarter of a million, wasn't it?"

"This is different. It's dynamite and we've got to keep it from going off. If something like this got out, the whole industry would suffer, not just me. Christ! a lot of us are feeling the inflation pinch the way it is. You know that. People don't go to concerts like they used to."

"Sure. So, you're going to have him locked up, right?"

"We'll decide what to do with him," Shapiro said with exaggerated patience, "if we find out who he is."

"What difference will that make? I won't be part of a coverup, Arn. I'll fly around and get your boys and girls out of jams, but I won't watch someone get away with murder. You should know that."

Shapiro leaned forward across the desk.

"Look, Steve, don't paint me as the villain of this piece. Don't you think I lay awake nights, telling myself

13

that the death of these last two girls rests on my soul? If I had just put the pieces of the puzzle together sooner. Or admitted the truth to myself sooner! Right now, I'm doing my best to make up for lost time. But we take it one step at a time."

"If you're right about the killer being one of those boys in the Tree, we're risking the life of every groupie that the band draws until we've got our nut tagged," said Madison. "I hear those boys like their fun. Plenty of ladies."

"So, you get on the job today," Shapiro said. "I've got you two seats booked on the eleven-thirty Continental flight to Chicago. You can join up with the tour at the hotel late this afternoon. The Tree is doing Soldier Field tonight."

"Why two seats on the plane? I don't want any company."

Shapiro picked up the interoffice phone on his desk.

"Connie, would you step in for a moment, please?" Replacing the receiver, he looked back at Madison. "I'm backing you on this one, Steve."

The door behind Madison opened. The receptionist from the outer, office stepped in.

Connie Frazer had caught Madison's eye on a number of previous visits to Arn's headquarters. But the visits were always fast, like this one. There had been no time for dates or getting acquainted. But it had not been due to lack of interest or hormonal response. No, indeed.

The lady was a fox.

She was about twenty-three, feminine yet confidant and self-possessed, dressed tastefully in a light tan slacks-and-jacket combination that followed every curve just so. Clear, piercing blue-green eyes met Madison's briefly. The only flaw in a lovely face of high, smooth cheekbones and aristocratically tilted nose was really no fault at all, as far as Madison was concerned. The lady's lower lip was perhaps a bit too full aesthetically, the mouth curving into a slight natural pout that suggested a most sensual nature.

"Yes, Arn?"

"Connie, I've told Steve that you'll be working this with him," Shapiro said. "Ready to leave?"

"I've got the tickets with me."

Shapiro turned to Madison.

"Steve, you and Connie are hooking up with the tour in Chicago as publicity liaison with this office. The band doesn't know that I've worked out the publicity with outfits in each of the cities, so you'll be covered. All you have to do is stay on top of the boys in the group and get to the bottom of this thing. I figure four eyes are better than two, so Connie's going with you." He started to rise. "Well, I guess you two had better be on your way if you're going to catch that plane. Connie was good enough to offer to drive to the airport, so—"

Madison lifted a hand.

"Whoa, Arn. Since when am I part of a team?" Shapiro gave the impression of being disconcerted

"What's Wrong, Steve? It'll look a lot better if someone from the office is along. The guys have seen Connie when they were up signing contracts. You won't have to worry about them finding out who you are."

"Wrong, Arn." Madison's eyes were narrow. The mouth was grim. "Let the word get out and they'd be the ones to worry. Maybe that's what you should do. Put the heat on and watch things jump."

"No, dammit," Shapiro almost snarled. "I told you I want you playing low-key on this one. You stay undercover until you've got something. Connie will keep your cover intact, that's all."

"Then you mean we're not working together, right? I want to make sure Connie's got the game-plan straight."

Connie's eyes flared. She was tired of standing on the sidelines.

. "I think Arn's taking me into confidence on this should account for something, Steve. We were going over the 'game-plan' while you were still on that flight from Denver. There will be a lot to keep an eye on if we're going to crack this, and it could happen a lot sooner if we worked together. Please don't go macho on us."

"I'll explain it to you sometime," Madison said, and ignored the even hotter flareup that brought. He looked back at Shapiro. "Let's talk price, Arn."

"What's wrong with the usual? Ten grand- plus expenses."

"Make it fifteen. I've got a feeling about this one. I think I'm going to earn it."

"Fifteen!?" Shapiro gasped. "Christ! No wonder you can afford a ranch in Colorado!"

"You said the deaths of some of those girls were resting on your soul," said Madison. "Maybe if they rested on your bank account, you'll be a little quicker on the uptake next time."

Shapiro reached for a checkbook and scribbled in it.

"Just what I need," he grumbled. "A wiseass conscience."

He tore the check from the book and handed it to Madison. Madison stood, slipping the check into his wallet.

"You're trying to play slick with me, Arn. It was your idea to make this job different from the others. The price goes up accordingly."

"Are you saying this job is different," asked Connie Frazer, "because Arn is sending someone along with you? Or because that someone is a woman?"

"Forget it," said Madison. "Arn's paid for his mistake. Let's book to the airport."

Shapiro's face clouded.

"Now remember, Steve. Very low profile, okay?"

"I'll be in touch," Madison promised.

He turned and left, not waiting for goodbyes or to make sure that the woman was behind him.

3

IT WAS A WARM, CLEAR SUMMER EVENING IN CHICAGO. Soldier Field, on the city's north side, was packed and still filling. Young people, most of them in their late teens and early twenties, were swarming through the turn-styles. A festive partying atmosphere was the order of the night. The early arrivals had commandeered the playing field itself with their blankets, crowding right up to the front of the elevated stage. Behind them, the stands too were nearly filled. The two lesser known warmup bands had come on and done their job, getting the audience excited and ready for the star attraction. Now a crew of roadies were busy hustling about the stage, getting the band's heavy equipment ready for performance. The electricity of expectation coursed through the crowd. Only another twenty minutes, a half hour at most, and it would be showtime.

The night, and the crowd, belonged to The Screaming Tree.

Steve Madison stood on the fringe of the crowd below the bleachers, taking it all in. The scent of pot and hash was so thick in the air, he wondered why he wasn't feeling-stoned just from walking around. But he was straight, and he planned to stay that way. Being stoned and working assignments for Arn Shapiro just didn't mix.

The energy from the young crowd had an exhilarating effect on him. It was its own special kind of high. He'd experienced it for the first time as a high-school boy in 1963 when he'd gone to see The Beatles on their first American tour. The British Invasion had followed. The Rolling Stones, The Animals, The Who and countless other young, angry, high-pressure Cockney bands. And Steve Madison, like most people of his age in America, had fallen totally, helplessly, happily in love with the sounds and lifestyle of rock 'n roll. In the years since, Madison, the world and his love affair with rock had all gone through many, many changes. But the love still burned.

After high school had come a brief, unsuccessful shot at college, then the Army. Vietnam. Then, upon discharge, his own rock band. Scuffling, trying to make it, and realizing ultimately that those Chosen few who did make it to the top were from the hundreds of thousands who were trying, and that to make it, somewhere along the line something had to be sacrificed to the almighty god of success. Sometimes it was integrity;

Sometimes it was your soul. Sometimes it was more. Janis and Jimi, among many others, had learned that the hard way. But whatever the price, Steve Madison had decided it was too high for success in such a mercurial profession. Some things weren't worth giving up, even for love. So now he was trouble-shooter-on- call for Arn Shapiro. Still a functioning unit of the exciting world of rock music, but master of his soul, his integrity, his life.

It was the only way Madison knew how to live.

He'd come out front tonight, as he always did when his assignments for Arn took him to concerts, to experience, however briefly, the hubbub and commotion of the expectant audience; of those who shared his love. Soldier Field pulsed with the vibes of *Now;* with the throbbing intensity of life itself. The sense of oneness that resulted among all these people was as much a part of Rock as the music itself.

Connie Frazer was backstage waiting for the Tree to arrive from their hotel. Madison had considered going directly up to their suite immediately upon his arrival in town and introducing himself under his cover as publicity coordinator. But after some more thought he'd decided against it, preferring instead to meet them this evening in a more casual, social setting at the gig where, as part of the flurry of everything else happening, he would draw less attention. This was The Screaming Tree's only performance in the Windy City. There would be a party, probably a wild party, back at the hotel after the performance. There would be plenty of time and opportunity to start nosing around then.

Onstage, most of the band's equipment was in place and ready. The small red indicator lights of the warming amplifiers, indicating that the juice was running, surveyed the crowd like hungry eyes. Everything was set but, showbiz being what it is no matter what the format, the audience would be kept waiting at least another fifteen minutes to build the suspense even further and enhance the moment when the Tree at last burst forth. But they would have arrived at the Field by now, and that's what Madison had been waiting for.

He began navigating his way around the perimeter of the mob, toward the backstage area. He found himself thinking about Connie Frazer, and their flight from New York.

It had been a generally pleasant flight. Pleasant because Connie Frazer was a lovely lady, and because the feminist chip she'd displayed on her shoulder in Aim's office had not surfaced again. Their conversation during the first part of the flight had consisted primarily of social niceties and comparing tastes in music and film.

It had taken her forty-five minutes to reach the bottom line.

"You said something in Arn's office that's been bothering me ever since," she'd said somewhere over Ohio.

He'd been expecting this. It had only been a matter of time.

"You mean about explaining my attitude?"

"Yes. Steve, since we've left his office we've touched on more subjects than I can count and I haven't discovered even a trace of male chauvinism."

"Why, thank you, ma'am."

"But when Arn told you I was coming along on this trip, you acted like the Threatened Male- incarnate."

"You just read the signs wrong, Connie," he told her. "I just don't like what Arn was trying to pull. I still don't."

"You mean backing you up on this?"

"It's more than that. I could handle this one on my own and Arn damn well knows it."

"Then why am I along?" she asked. "I don't like people playing games with me."

"Then you shouldn't be working for Arn Shapiro. You really don't know why he sent you along?"

"Why don't you tell me?'

"Okay. Arn and I see eye-to-eye because I get results. He used to manage a band I was in and when I hung up my rock' n roll shoes he offered me the job I've got now. On every assignment he's tossed me so far, I've come up smelling of roses. But this job is different from the others. Way different. It's not angling one of his acts out from under a sticky personal mess or a good talent being wasted by drugs. Like Arn said, it's dynamite."

"What will he do if he's right and someone in the Tree is involved in those murders?'

"I don't know. I don't think Arn knows, himself. But whatever it is, he wants to make the decision."

Intelligent, feminine eyes glinted with awareness. "And that's where I come in?',

Madison nodded. "You're along to keep your eyes on yours truly as well as on the members of The Screaming Tree," he said. "Arn wants to know if I start getting religion. If I start thinking about justice instead of his bank account."

"Arn wouldn't let someone get away with murder.".

"Yeah, that's what he says. What he'd probably like to do is have me find out who it is and then have the guy quietly whisked away into a mental institution. Arn's afraid I might find out which one of the Tree is killing young girls and blow the guy's brains out—and the whole thing sky-high at the same time."

"Would you?",

"I might, if I knew for a fact that I had my man."

Connie shivered. The rapport between them that had been building since Shapiro's office was dying fast.

"That's pretty brutal, isn't it?"

"But effective.".

"But what gives you the right to take another man's life like that?",

"What gives some man the right to kill those four girls? Or doesn't that matter because they were dumb groupies and the man's part of a million-dollar rock act?"

Now the eyes glinted with something else. "You know that isn't what I meant," she said. "But the law—"

"—will put him in the funny farm for a few years until he's 'sane' again. *If* they work hard and get lucky and find all the proof they need, which they won't. I couldn't live with that, Connie. I value human life too damn much. Even a groupie's life."

"So, what you're saying is, Arn is right. He does need to watchdog you."

"No one's going to stop me from doing what I have to do," he told her.

He'd said it firmly, but not as a threat or a promise... it was merely fact.

It was also the end of the conversation. She hadn't spoken again until they were approaching O'Hare, and then it was back to the niceties and pleasantries. The rapport had indeed been broken.

Madison couldn't blame her. He'd given Connie Frazer plenty to think about. He had his own share of food for thought, too. Such as: What if Shapiro was totally off-base about a connection between the murders and the band? And if he wasn't, what *would* Madison do?

Steve Madison knew he'd have to play it as he played life—as it came.

The area surrounding the backstage entrance was crowded with milling kids, all trying to talk their way past the mountainous uniformed rent-a-cop who blocked the doorway with his arms folded. Some of the kids wanted back in a big way, to hobnob with the

stars. One was saying he had designed some clothes he
wanted to show to Mick Adamson, the lead singer.
Another said he was Adamson's brother: He was
flashing a driver's license. A young woman said she was
one of Mick's best friends. He'd asked her to come
down but must have forgotten to leave word at the
door. It all came at the rent-a-cop at once, part of the
larger, constant barrage of the stadium. But he had his
orders to keep *everyone* without a Stage Pass *out*. He
only glanced away from the hassling kids for a moment
to look at Madison's I.D. His nod sent Madison on into
the Fantasy World itself.

The labyrinth of narrow, low-ceilinged corridors
which led to The Screaming Tree's dressing room was
filled over capacity by members of the two warmup
bands and their considerable assemblage of hangers-
on. The place was wall-to-wall people, crackling with
excitement. Madison brought his elbow into use and
began plowing through. The closer he came to the
dressing room, the thicker the crowd got.

The reason these two bands were chosen to open
the show was that they were nearly as apt to launch as
The Tree themselves. It was like a circus back there.
Like a gala masquerade party at some home for the
incurably weird.

One guy was stark naked, his body aglow with
filled-in circles of loud paint and sparkling sequins
pasted across his hips and penis. No one seemed to
notice him. Every once in a while, someone clasping a
guitar, or a set of drumsticks would stumble by, drip-

ping with perspiration, chest pumping, winding down from the adrenaline rush that had kept him going for the last sixty minutes. Over in a comer, an angry white girl was screaming at one of the black musicians.

"You bastard! No one leaves me stuck in a hotel room like that!"

"Baby, you was out! I tried to wake you, I swear. But you wouldn't move and the limos were leavin'."

"Don't give me that crap! You didn't even pay the bill, you cheap bastard. I don't know a soul in Miami Beach. What the hell was I supposed to do for money?"

"Baby, don't forget how I met you in Tulsa. What's wrong with what you *been* doin', bitch?'

Madison spotted Connie Frazer through a sea of bobbing heads. She was beckoning him. With a final effort, he elbowed his way through to her.

"They just got here," she reported. "But no one can get through. Believe me, I tried. Even Arn's name doesn't help. The only person in or out is Lee Brocchi, and such a wall you never saw. Plus, he's got two rent-a-cops on the door with him.'"

Brocchi was the band's road manager and bodyguard.

"He knows you, doesn't he?' asked Madison.

"Of course, he does. They all do, from the times they've been up to the office. But I guess the band decided to put themselves off bounds until after the show."

Madison moved past her.

"Let's try it again," he said.

STEPHEN MERTZ

"Steve, maybe we should wait until the party at the hotel to see them," she said, keeping pace at his side. "We don't want to draw too much attention to ourselves."

"Sure we do," grinned Madison. "Follow my lead."

Then they were at the door of the dressing room. Madison had no trouble in getting one of the uniformed guards to fetch Brocchi.

The Screaming Tree's road honcho stood about five-nine, stockily built, with super-wide shoulders, a tanned complexion, and short hair and intense eyes that were both cold and dark. He didn't look friendly.

"You wanted something?" he asked Madison.

"I want Mick, Jeremy and Keith," Madison told him. "I'm supposed to be coordinating their publicity on this tour."

"So, coordinate. This is a gig. You're not needed here."

He started to turn.

Madison said, softly, "Just tell them one of the girls in Cleveland sent me with a message." Brocchi's body seemed to tighten.

"What the hell's that supposed to mean?"

"Just tell them, Lee."

"Tell which one?"

"Hell, I don't give a damn. Use your own judgment. You're the man in charge here. There was a party last night in Cleveland, right? There were a lot of girls there. Just tell the guys what I said."

Their eyes locked and held for long seconds. Then

28

Brocchi turned and disappeared back into the dressing room.

Connie Frazer cleared her throat.

"Thanks for hashing that one over with me the way you did, Steve. I'm glad we're working together on this thing."

"I couldn't have you running off to call Arn," Madison said. "I needed to get this far."

The door opened. Brocchi stepped back into the corridor.

"Alright, come on in," he said curtly. "Say what you came for, and then get the hell out."

"One question, Lee," said Madison. "Which one gave the high sign to let me in?'

Brocchi paused, one hand on the doorknob. "What's the difference?"

"No difference. So why not tell me?"

"So, it was Jeremy who said to let you in and the others said okay, too. Okay, question-man?"

"Okay," said Madison.

He and Connie entered the dressing room. Brocchi stepped in behind them.

Madison took the room and the people in it at a glance, registering as much as he could. The room was a microcosm of the rock insanity outside.

The three members of The Screaming Tree, all in their early to mid-twenties, were done out head to foot in extravagant black leather jumpsuits, high-heeled platform boots, silver slashes or iridescent "lighting" lacing out across their costumes, and wild, darkly painted faces beneath frizzed-out, wildly dyed, sequined hair. Madison had seen their pictures often enough in the rock media not to need introductions.

Jeremy Bates, vocal and guitar. A narrow-built guy with an almost boyish smile that somehow made it through all the layers of paint and makeup.

A slender, gentle-looking lady, about the same age as Jeremy, balanced on one of his knees with her arm loosely around his neck. She had long dark hair and brown eyes and was dressed in faded Levis and a sweater. But somehow, she didn't seem out of place with the wild man beneath her.

Her eyes met Madison's briefly, flickered, then looked away.

She was Laura Bates. Mrs. Jeremy.

Keith Terrance, powerhouse drummer, was slumped down in laid-back comfort on a plastic couch. He was a hulking six-feet-plus. Even in repose there was about him the aura of a timebomb waiting to explode. He watched Madison silently with lazy eyes that said nothing.

Mick Adamson, lead vocals and bass, was another matter. The compact, wiry, rubber-lipped singer sat on the edge of the makeup table. He was high on something, or maybe he was just getting wound up for the show. There was a jerky, almost squirrelly manner about him. His white knuckles gripped the table's edge.

Jeremy Bates studied Madison from around his wife. His spacey, good natured smile was still in place.

"And here's the man with the message from Cleveland," he said. He gave a wave to Connie Frazer. "Hey, Connie, how 'ya doing? Sorry about the blockade. Lee was just following orders. It's kind of nice to be alone just before a gig and, uh, you know—" He held two fingers to his right nostril and sniffed loudly. "—get relaxed before we go on."

"Or whatever you wanna call it," laughed Adamson.

"I understand," said Connie. "It's just that I brought along a new face on the tour and Arn thought it might be good if I introduced him to you right away."

"And I was so anxious to meet the big stars myself, Connie, don't forget that," Madison added.

He caught her warning glance but didn't have time to acknowledge it. Hulking Keith Terrance climbed to his feet from the couch.

"Is that supposed to be funny, man?' he wanted to know. "Who the fuck are you, Johnny Carson?"

Madison told him his name. "Sit down, Keith," he added quietly. "Save it for the fans. I'm not into prima donna trips."

The timebomb exploded. Keith Terrance lunged forward, like some loping demon in his getup. A meaty, calloused hand plowed into Madison's shoulder, jarring him back.

"No one gives a shit what you're into, man," the drummer hissed. "You wanted to come back here so goddamn much. All right, you came back. You seen the stars. Now blow before I lay some real stars on you."

He laughed at what he thought was a joke. Jeremy

STEPHEN MERTZ

Bates made a sound with his mouth that was half annoyance and half disgust.

"Come on, Keith. Give the guy a break. You don't have to prove anything."

From the makeup table, Mick Adamson laughed too, and the almost giggly nature of the laugh confirmed something Madison had guessed. The guy was wired out of his mind on something. Probably speed. "Come on yourself, Jeremy," he snorted. "Go on, Keith. Give this bastard the bum's rush." He shifted his wild gaze and raped Connie Frazer with his eyes. "The lady can stay."

"You hear that, dude?" Terrance demanded. "It's two to one and majority rules in this here band. Now buy a ticket the hell out of here while you can still walk."

"Jeremy's right," Madison said. "You don't have to prove anything, Keith. You've got nothing *to* prove."

Keith Terrance did just what Madison wanted him to do. With an outraged roar he lunged forward again, both big hands coming up now and reaching for Madison's throat. Madison jerked his own right hand up so quickly that the movement was a blur. He got the drummer's right wrist between his thumb and first two fingers and gave a quick twist. It was a move he hadn't used since Nam. Terrance screamed and spun away, his face contorted with pain. He fell to the couch holding his wrist between his legs, rocking like a man having a fit.

Brocchi snarled something and darted forward,

crouching down before Terrance and trying to get a look at the wrist.

"My wrist!" Terrance was screaming to nobody in particular. "The bastard broke my goddamn wrist!"

Terrance's conniptions were too animated for Brocchi to get through. The road manager looked back Over his shoulder, his eyes blazing. "What the hell did you have to do that for?' he demanded. "If Keith can't play tonight, you're dead, mister. I don't care if you're working for Jesus Christ.".

"Relax," said Madison. "I just pinched a nerve to calm him down a little. I leave when I want to leave." He looked at Jeremy Bates. "You didn't ask which girl in Cleveland sent the message," he said.

Bates glanced at Keith Terrance and there seemed something like satisfaction in the smile he shot back at Madison.

"You didn't give me much time. Not that I'm complaining. Keith's needed that for quite a while."

"Right. So, I'm giving you time now." He pointedly ignored Mrs. Bates. "Not interested?"

Bates flashed his good-natured smile again.

"Not especially. I don't even know any girls in Cleveland." He gave the lady on his knee a hug. "My woman's right here and she's all I need. Mick and Keith didn't seem to react so I figured it was some kind of hustle. Thought it might be interesting. So okay, man. Is it a hustle? Is there some girl in Cleveland with a message?'

Madison gave the guy a smile in return.

"I guess not. I guess I really did just want to meet the big stars."

On the couch, Keith Terrance had stopped making so much noise. But that didn't help Brocchi's mood any.

"Well now that you've seen them, why don't you take Keith's advice and get the hell out of here," he said tightly. "You've got a job to do and it damn well doesn't include pushing these guys around."

Terrance looked at Madison. He was blinking away the last of his pain tears.

"You're lucky I've got a show to do, dude. You stay away from me on this tour. You even look at me the wrong way and I'm gonna use my knife."

Mick Adamson seemed oblivious to the drama before him. He was still undressing Connie Frazer with slightly out-of-focus eyes.

"But you can stay, Connie," he reminded her hotly. "This is a real fun band—and the fun don't start until after the show, right Keith?'

"Speaking of shows, maybe you'd better blow, Steve," said Jeremy Bates. "There's a few thousand people waiting for us out there. We'd better earn our bread."

"I'll be at the party tonight," Madison promised the room in general. "Let's continue the party then, shall we? I'll try not to scare myself to death worrying about Keith in the meantime."

Jeremy Bates chuckled at that. Laura Bates was looking blankly at the opposite wall, as if removing herself from everything. Terrance, Adamson and Brocchi just glared, waiting for the intruder to leave.

Madison turned, and Connie followed him out into the crowded corridor. The door slammed behind them with finality. Madison clasped the lady's hand and with some effort they navigated their way through the sea of craziness toward the Field once again.

When they were back outside, she said, "You don't believe much in making good first impressions, do you? Jesus! Arn would have a cardiac arrest if he saw you treating his stars like that."

"The only way to get things cooking is to turn on the heat," Madison told her.

"Well, I guess I'm in it with you now," she sighed. "I convinced them we were bosom buddies the first time I tried to get in. I'm sure I'm on their hate list how, too. Thanks a lot."

"Bosom buddies, huh?"

"So, since we're in it, why don't we discuss it," she suggested. "It would be kind of unique keeping up with you for a change. You've met the band. Any ideas?"

"It's too early for ideas. The recipe calls for more stirring. I kind of hope it isn't Jeremy, if it's any of them."

"His wife sure gave you a funny look when we came in, Steve. Like she knew you."

"Must have been my potent virility. I'm a Taurus, you know."

"Must have been. Well, don't pass Jeremy Bates by as a suspect just because of that nice-guy smile. He comes across like Mr. Mellow—but underneath he's twice the sadistic bastard of those other two put together."

Madison arched an eyebrow.

"Is that the voice of experience speaking?'

"Uh-huh. Sometime, when we know each other a little better, I'll show you the scars."

That was enough for Madison. He didn't push it. There wasn't time even if he'd wanted to. The stadium lights dimmed and three bright spotlights picked out three points on the stage. He and Connie moved in as best they could. An expectant hush had fallen over the crowd. It would be less than a minute to showtime.

But Steve Madison wasn't thinking about rock concerts at the moment. Not even this one. His mind was busy sorting and filing for future reference the kaleidoscope of impressions which he'd carried with him from The Screaming Tree's dressing room. Not to mention the tidbit Connie Frazer had just tossed his way. But even all that took backseat to the biggest surprise he'd received.

Connie Frazer was a sharp woman. She'd read the signals correctly. Laura Bates had recognized Steve Madison. And Madison had recognized her. Why shouldn't he? He never forgot ex-lovers. Especially ones that had meant as much to him as Laura. Two summers ago, her name had been Laura Hagen...

Then, abruptly, the show began. A near- hysterical announcer shouted the band's name over the P A. Jeremy Bates, Keith Terrance and Mick Adamson charged onstage, Terrance to his drumkit and Jeremy and Mick to plug the cords of their guitars into their amplifiers.

The rising roar of sixty thousand screaming, whistling fans crashed in over Madison like a breaking wave.

4

THE POST-CONCERT PARTY WAS JUST GETTING UNDER way when Steve Madison and Connie Frazer arrived. Madison's ears were still ringing. The Screaming Tree's performance at Soldier Field had been a ninety-minute blitzkrieg upon the senses. An extravaganza of thundering music, exploding smoke-bombs and multi-colored strobe lights. Keith Terrance had propelled the group with his high-pressure drumming while Jeremy Bates and Mick Adamson had been all over the stage, Adamson screaming the occult-oriented lyrics, backed by the booming wall of sound, taking the crowd higher and higher until the show had climaxed with the Tree's current hit, *Lucifer's Calling*.

Subtlety wasn't the Tree's thing. Their performance had been primal yet professional. Their commitment, apparently total. The audience had filed out looking exhausted, happy and satisfied. They'd gotten their money's worth.

Arriving back at the hotel, Madison made one short stop before he and Connie joined the festivities downstairs. He detoured into his room and slipped his shoulder holster on under his jacket. The holster was specially designed to be worn under casual clothes and held a heavy .44 Magnum with a six- inch barrel. Connie watched, saying nothing.

Laura Bates was the first person Madison recognized upon entering the dining room where the party was being held. She didn't see him. She and Lee Brocchi were standing at the far end of a long table lined with food and drink. They were discussing something in earnest. Brocchi's face seemed etched with attentive concern.

The party was being tossed by the local concert promoter. The Screaming Tree hadn't shown up yet but the media people, the two warmup bands and their parties were all there in full force, enthusiastically imbibing of the provided freebies. The black musician and his lady friend from Soldier Field must have made up. They strolled up holding hands, smiling. A number of the rock press were busy earning their pay. Several interviews were in progress in various parts of the room while mellow jazz wafted from a hidden sound system. New faces were still arriving. The atmosphere was friendly and relaxed against a constant backdrop of rippling conversation and clinking glasses.

"What now, chief?' asked Connie after Madison had fetched them drinks.

They stood by the wall nearest the doorway, across

the room from Laura and Brocchi. "When the band shows up, we stay on top of them," Madison replied. "Anyone leaves,' we follow."

"There are three of them and two of us. What if they all leave and split up? What if one of them leaves before coming down to the party?"

"Then we ad-lib. And there aren't three. There are four. You're forgetting Brocchi."

"Lee?" She shook her head. "Come on, Steve. He's the only normal one in the bunch. He was just coming on strong at the gig because you were. He is their bodyguard."

"Which means he was with them in every city where one of those girls died."

Across the room, Brocchi excused himself to Laura Bates. He finished his drink and left the room, passing Madison and Connie with a nod and said nothing. After he was gone, Laura surveyed the crowd for the first time since Madison had entered. Her brown eyes rested on him immediately. Then she got busy refreshing her drink.

"Mrs. Bates seems strongly affected by that Taurian virility," Connie commented.

Madison laughed.

"You don't miss much, lady. Keep your eyes open. It's time to play detective."

He didn't wait for a reply. He edged his way through the crowd. Laura Bates saw him coming, but she was between the table and the wall with no place to go, and he was closing fast. Then he was beside her.

"Hello, Laura."

"Steve—"

"It was a surprise to run into you. I knew Jeremy was married, but that side was always played down in the publicity. How have you been?'

She looked down.

"It hurts to see you again, Steve. I don't know why that is after all this time. It's been nearly two years."

"It seems longer in some ways, and shorter in others," said Madison. "You were the stringer for *Rolling Stone* and I was the hungry musician on his way up."

"I had to get away from the music for a while after we split," she said. "It hurt too much to even think about it because then I'd think of you."

"I thought I was tying you down, Laura. I'm not so sure now if I was, but that's all past now anyway, isn't it?'

"I could have been so happy with you, Steve," she said. "I wanted to be your woman so bad."

"Does Jeremy know about us?"

"No. Past lovers are something we don't talk about, It's a mutual agreement."

"I hear he likes to play rough sometimes."

"He's a complicated man. What was that hassle in the dressing room about, Steve?"

"What did Jeremy say it was about? He didn't say, and I didn't ask."

"Worried about a girl in Cleveland? What about the mutual agreement?"

She began to say something in anger, then caught herself.'

"Why don't we just stay away from each other, alright? You know too much about me. You know where all the weak spots are. You messed up my life once, Steve. And once was enough."

"I'm here on a job, Laura," he told her. "I'll see that it stays that way."

They both picked up the movement of someone approaching. Lee Brocchi and Jeremy Bates were crossing the room toward them.

The party had picked up steam. Late arrivals were still pouring in. At the far side of the room Madison could see Keith Terrance and Mick Adamson. They were standing side by side, fielding questions from a local reporter. Withouthis makeup, Terrance looked like a huge, relaxed bear. Adamson didn't seem as wired as at the gig. He was drinking a soda. Connie Frazer was with a group of people standing nearby. She seemed to have that front covered.

Jeremy Bates, *sans* makeup, was as mild and friendly as before.

"How'd you like the show?" he asked Madison as he and Brocchi came up. He slid an arm around Laura's waist, drawing her to him possessively. "Is this the first time you've seen the band play?"

"Pretty good, and yes," said Madison. "That's some powerful material. Who writes your stuff?"

"We all do, in a way. I supply the rhythms and

melodies, and Mick and Keith come up with the words."

"I hate to say this, but you don't exactly come across as the satanic type, Jeremy."

Laura said, "The occult stuff is all Mick and Keith's. They're into that trip real heavy. But they needed music for their lyrics."

Brocchi joined the conversation.

"They ran into Jeremy and he came up with all the right sounds," he said with a trace of pride. "The group clicked, and people are hot for them, so Jeremy's riding it out."

"But I'm not about to start attending any black masses," Jeremy laughed. "Straight religion is scary enough for me. As far as Satanism goes, I'm blissfully ignorant."

How about you?" Laura asked Madison.

"Just for the dollar sign." He replied.

"Hell, aren't we all? I came in with Jeremy. I mother-henned the last bunch of rowdies he was with." He looked at Jeremy as if provoking another round in a longstanding argument. "But those rowdies were a helluva lot easier to take than these loonies."

Jeremy laughed.

"And the paycheck was a helluva lot smaller." He gave his wife a lover's hug. "Come on, babe. Let's go hunt up some drinks."

They moved off down the table. Madison's eyes followed them.

"He must soothe over a lot of hassles with that smile," he said.

"I have some soothing over to do myself," said Brocchi. He'd lost all the hard coldness that Madison had run up against in the dressing room. "I guess I overreacted earlier tonight. Things get crazy right before a gig. The band told me to keep everyone out. I guess I should have made an exception in your case."

"Forget it. I was a little hyper, myself."

Brocchi's face clouded. "Now I hope you can straighten things out with Keith," he said. "Sometimes that boy comes on too damn strong for his own good."

Madison did a quick visual pan of the still growing party. Some more girls had arrived. Groupies, all arched breasts, provocative smiles and plenty of leg. Three of them had latched onto Keith. The drummer was in his glory. He was a good-looking guy without the stage makeup. Heavy on the brawn, hold the brains. The girls thought he was terrific.

Mick Adamson was standing in a group that included record execs and Connie Frazer. Madison caught Connie's eye from across the room, and she nodded slightly.

He looked at Brocchi. "Terrance said something about using a knife on me. Anything to it?"

"He's a brawler," said Brocchi. "He and Mick grew up together—tough. They became rock stars, but they still like to bust heads. We can't work Dallas anymore because Keith decked a cop the last time they played there. Just go easy around him. Everything'll be cool."

"Right. I'll try to behave myself."

You could feel Brocchi's body temperature begin to drop. Some of the hardness was coming back.

"Who are you?' he growled. "You don't kiss ass enough to be a promo man, and you ask too many questions. What are you doing, setting one of us up for a bust?"

Movement caught the corner of Madison's eye. It was Keith Terrance. The drummer was heading toward the exit and he had depleted the groupie's ranks by one. He had his arm around a willowy blonde girl, and they weren't wasting any time.

Madison started after them. He hadn't expected things to click this fast.

"Have Arn explain it," he said to Brocchi. "If you haven't figured it out already."

Brocchi looked like he was going to follow at first, but Shapiro's name started him thinking. Across the room, Terrance and his new girlfriend disappeared through the exit. Laughing, yapping people with drinks blocked Madison's way. By the time he reached the exit, Connie Frazier was there waiting for him.

"You're leaving me with my hands full," she whispered, not frantic but getting there.

"Just do your best to keep track of everyone," said Madison. "If Brocchi starts asking questions, you don't know anything. Have him call Arn."

"Steve, maybe you should call the police."

"Why? Because Keith Terrance picked up a groupie? Look, what's the next stop on the tour?"

"Kansas City."

"Okay. If you haven't heard from me by tomorrow night, you get in touch with Arn, too."

Her breasts lifted as she caught her breath. That sensuous lower lip trembled, only it wasn't passion. It was worry. "What should I tell him? Where will you be?'

Madison started past her, out the door. "Missing in action," he said.

He regretted the words as soon as they came out. It was intended to bring a laugh, but it only brought a wince and more worry. He wanted to say some more but there was no time. Down the hallway he could make out Keith Terrance and the girl crossing the lobby toward the street entrance.

Madison left the dining room and followed them into the night.

5

KEITH TERRANCE AND HIS LADY FRIEND CAUGHT A CAB from the line in front of the hotel. Steve Madison waited until they were halfway down the block. Then he left the front entrance and grabbed the next cab in line.

"Follow the cab that just took off," he instructed the driver.

The driver was a college age kid with round glasses, acne and wild hair down to his shoulders.

"You're kidding. What is this, a movie?"

Terrance's cab was pulling onto Michigan, heading north. Madison drew out his wallet and flashed a twenty under the kid's nose.

"Lights, camera, action," he said. "You're losing them."

The cab slipped into gear and pulled away from the curb. Traffic was light. By the time Terrance's cab had merged with the northbound flow on Lake Shore

Drive, Madison's driver had fallen in behind at a comfortable distance. Madison settled back in his seat. His knowledge of Chicago's layout was sketchy and mostly limited to the Loop. After some two miles the first taxi cut west and after two more turns Madison gave up trying to keep track of where they were.

Terrance had his driver pull up at midblock on a dark, treelined residential street and he and the blonde disembarked. The summer night was still; the sounds of the city muffled and distant. Madison's driver parked a half-block back and killed his lights.

Up ahead, the first cab pulled away. Terrance and the girl followed the short walk up to the house. The taxi ride hadn't cooled them down any. They were all over each other even as they walked, their shadows becoming one as they stood on the stoop while the lady looked for her key.

Madison gave his driver the twenty and started to slide out.

"I'll take it from here. Thanks."

The boy seemed strangely reluctant to take the tip. He sized Madison up one last time, then reached over the seat, proffering a thickly rolled joint.

"Not that this is a regular service of the company or anything," he grinned, "but if that's your old lady maybe you'd better cool down a little first. I hate to see people get in trouble."

Madison slammed the door after him.

"And I always thought Chicago was an unfriendly town. Don't worry, I'm just going to watch."

The joint disappeared.

"Oh. A kinko, huh?"

The lights came on and the cab pulled away from the curb.

Madison started toward the house into which Terrance and the blonde had disappeared. His footsteps echoed on the sidewalk. Incongruously, thoughts and images of Colorado came to his mind—packing a sleeping bag and a week's provisions and riding up above the timberline. The city as foreign to Madison as Vietnam had been. And he would have to be every bit as cautious in this jungle as he had been in that one. He pushed the images of home from his consciousness.

It was an old neighborhood. The houses that lined both sides-on the street, each of them less than ten feet from the other, were bulky, dark shadows in the gloom. The hour was late. The street slept.

Unlike the houses on either side of it, the one into which Terrance had gone was a one-story structure.

As Madison approached, a light went on midway back. A narrow, paved walkway led between this house and the one next to it, leading directly beneath the square of illumination. The house next door was as silent and asleep as all the others on the block and Madison hoped it would stay that way. It would be hell to be dragged in as a peeping tom.

He moved toward the window. The ledge was even with his line of vision. The bottom of the shade stopped a half inch short of the sill and while Madison couldn't see much, he could see the old wrought iron bed and the area around it, and that was enough. The window was open a crack and he could hear too.

Keith Terrance had just flung himself onto his back on the bed. He was grinning in anticipation and reaching out with both arms.

"Come on, baby. Let's get down. It's late and I'll be gone on the ten o'clock flight."

That was Terrance. Simple and direct. And the girl thought it was great. Her laughter was stoned and musical.

"Don't be in too much of a hurry, daddy. Half the fun is getting there. I enjoyed your show tonight. Tell me what you think of mine."

That was the kind of invitation that Madison always had a hard time refusing. He shifted slightly, and his narrow line of vision took in the girl. He hadn't paid much attention to her until now. But then, the show was just getting started.

She was a big, healthy girl with a wholesome sexuality that is rare among backstage ladies. And there wasn't an ounce of misplaced flesh anywhere. She crossed her arms and pulled off her blouse, mussing her full blonde hair. She wore no bra and firm, hard-nippled breasts bounced and quivered with newfound freedom. All the time her hips were swaying back and forth as if she could still hear The Screaming Tree's music. She latched her thumbs in the waists of the slacks and pushed them down. The panties went with them.

Nude, glorious and willing, she approached the bed.

Right about now, Madison's conscience was beginning to bother him. He was enough of an old-time romantic to want to leave the two of them alone to their joy of sex. He had seen some skin of a very foxy lady, he was man enough to enjoy it and honest enough to admit that, but now there was a strong wish to walk until he hit a main stem and catch a cab back downtown.

But there was the job. He thought about that as the girl began undressing Terrance. The drummer was running idle fingers through her hair as she worked off his clothes. There was a smugness to his smile that the happy girl couldn't see as she labored.

It seemed to be stretching things a bit to expect the nut in the band—if there was one—to strike again so soon after killing the girl in Cleveland. He'd hit four times in the last year all over the globe and while that was a busy enough schedule, it seemed against the law of averages he'd decide to play Count Dracula twice in only three evenings.

Still, the murder in Cleveland had been a sex crime and there'd been no sign of a struggle. The girl in Cleveland had been getting it on with someone in the band just as the blonde girl was now.

He brought his eyes back to the action on the bed. She was just unbuckling Terrance's belt.

The doorbell rang.

Keith Terrance growled something about who the fuck could it be at this hour—and was answered as the person out on the front porch gave up on the bell and started pounding hell out of the door.

"Keith! Keith, open-up for Chrissake! I think you're being set up for a bust. Come on!"

It was Lee Brocchi's voice. He didn't seem to care if anyone in the neighborhood should wake up and hear him.

The blonde girl went to a closet and came back with a robe which she wrapped around those nice curves. Keith Terrance re-buckled his belt and pushed himself to his feet, his face a mask of anger.

"Keep it warm, Baby. I'll be right back."

He launched into a stream of fresh obscenities as he stomped from the bedroom. Brocchi resumed pounding louder than before, not sure if he'd been heard._

Madison left the window and moved softly back toward the front of the house. He must have kept perfect time with Terrance. He peered around the corner of the wall just as the front door was yanked open.

"Brocchi, what the goddamn hell—"

The bodyguard's manner was brisk and efficient. "Get your clothes on," he said hurriedly. "We're getting the hell out of here."

"The hell we are. Not with the nice piece of ass I got waiting for me back there. What are you on, man?"

"I'm a helluva lot straighter than you are," snapped Brocchi. "And think about your own ass for a change. Now do what I tell you and *move!*

The drummer was starting to buy that something was really wrong.

"What're you talking about a bust?"

Brocchi touched the guy's arm and started easing him back inside.

"I'll tell you about it while you get yourself together," he said.

The front door closed behind them, blocking out the rest of their conversation. Madison looked out into the street. A taxi cab sat at the curb in front of the house, its motor idling. He turned and started back toward the window. Things were starting to happen now. It was that stage of an assignment where it was all you could do to hold on and see where people and events would take you. He'd turned up the heat and stirred and yes, things were beginning to cook.

They stopped cooking abruptly.

He'd been too single-minded, he realized later. Too damn intent on the happenings within that house to be as careful as he should have been out there in the darkness where the jungle was deadliest.

He heard the blow before it struck. He knew in that last instant of thought that someone had come from the shadows of that other house.

Now that the knowledge registered—it was useless.

The violent blow slammed him behind his right ear and he knew nothing else. His body pitched to the walk. His mind exploded into unconsciousness...

The first thing he saw upon regaining consciousness were the two wide blue eyes staring back into his own. Awareness returned slowly by degrees and with awareness came pain. A dull, throbbing ache at first, then blistering needles all over but centered primarily between the temples.

The blue eyes didn't blink, didn't move.

They were less than twelve inches from his own. The fact that they did nothing but stare, told Madison intuitively that they belonged to a corpse.

He realized that he was lying on a bare wood floor, on his right side. The corpse had been stretched out alongside him, facing him.

He sat up.

It was the blonde girl.

He was too groggy and nauseous to be shocked. The room around him tilted but didn't go into a spin. He dropped his head forward and it cleared. This was the girl's bedroom. He recognized the wrought iron bed. A clutter on the table alongside the bed caught his eye: a bent spoon, candle, vials— a whole kit for shooting smack. Mutli-colored pills were scattered all over the place: on the table, the bed, across the floor, everywhere.

He groaned and reached for his gun. It was still there under his jacket. That was enough for now. He left it holstered and tried to set his mind in order. Impressions of movement while he'd been unconscious drifted to him like vague memories of a mostly forgotten dream. He didn't know how long he'd been out. He glanced at the window. It was still night.

Then he knew what had pulled him around again.

Somebody was pounding at the front door. The officious, authoritative rapping of someone who wanted in and wasn't about to wait much longer.

Through the narrow crack of the open bedroom window, through the stillness of early morning, came the static crackle of a police car radio. Then the sound of footfalls on the sidewalk between the houses. Heading for the back, trying to keep quiet. Moving fast.

Madison climbed to his feet. His eyes returned to the girl. Deep purple bruises circled her throat. You could still make out the fingermarks. Someone had choked her and smashed her head against the hard, wooden floor. The back of her head was a pulpy mess.

He turned and stepped into the narrow hallway that ran the length of the house. Someone was kicking at the front door now, just above the lock, trying to smash it in. Madison pulled out the .44 and threw a round at the door, aiming high. The report blasted the confines of the hall like a baby howitzer and a jagged hole the diameter of a good-sized punched itself through the thick slab of wood inches above head level.

Feet scurried, diving for cover.

Madison stalked toward the back of the house, formulating his strategy as he moved. The next room down from the bedroom featured a picture window facing onto the backyard of the house next door.

Madison didn't miss a beat. He dove through the plate glass with his arms crossed over his face, keeping his body loose, to the accompaniment of a splash-like shattering sound and millions of flying shards of glass.

He hit the ground beyond in a roll and came up running. He hefted the Magnum skyward as he ran, snapping off two more rounds. Then he was around the corner of the house and hauling ass down a narrow alley.

There was a report from somewhere back there. They were firing at shadows. But it wouldn't take them long to get on the radio if they hadn't already.

Madison skidded to a stop when he reached the street. The street was dark, silent; lined with parked cars. The closest was a VW bug. Madison holstered the .44. He approached the bug and got to work. It took him less than thirty seconds to successfully cross the wires. The little engine burst to life.

He climbed in and got the hell out of there.

He caught a main artery and traveled east until he reached North Clark. By now he had his bearings again. He steered the VW south toward the Loop and kept his speed down as he tooled through the sparse, sleepy traffic.

He was vaguely aware of the slivers of glass that covered him, but not much more. He only knew that he felt like a man bursting to the surface after being too long underwater, drawing in the fresh air, free once again...

Arn Shapiro had been right. There could be no doubt now. There was a killer on The Screaming Tree's tour. A killer who was perfectly willing to dust a human life simply to tangle Madison up and keep him from asking any more questions.

It would be a pleasure to waste the bastard.

Madison got one more turnaround that night, or morning. It happened after he had parked the VW, shook most of the glass shards from his clothes and walked the three blocks back to the hotel. It came as he was crossing the parking lot.

He had almost reached a densely shadowed rear entrance when a car pulled into a vacant parking space a few yards to his left. He gave the car an idle glance, then pulled up short as Mick Adamson climbed from behind the wheel. The Screaming Tree's lead singer circled around and held open the other door for his passenger, and Laura Bates stepped out.

She stepped out—and into Adamson's arms. Their mouths met hotly, and they merged into a clinch that was R-rated, at least.

Madison melted back into the shadows, watching.

Laura was glued to Adamson. Adamson's hands were busy. A muffled gasp of pleasure drifted to Madison amid the night sounds of the city.

Madison felt a strange empty sort of hurt wash over him. Then he thought of the dead blonde girl and her staring blue eyes and her bloody, smashed-in head...and he decided the hell with it.

Finding out that a lady he'd cared about was really no lady at all suddenly didn't seem so important after everything else that had gone down that evening.

He turned and entered the hotel. Seeing that the post-concert party was over, he caught an automatic elevator up to Connie Frazer's floor.

6

CONNIE FRAZER TOOK A FINAL TOKE ON THE JOINT, leaned over and snubbed it out in the coffee table ashtray. She looked back at Madison with a smile.

"Feeling better?" she asked.

They were in her room sharing a couch that looked over Chicago at night. Lake Michigan was an endless, inky blur beyond the lights of the city. Madison had broken his general rule of abstinence from the weed while working. One glance at the shape he was in and Connie had insisted, and Connie Frazer was far too good-looking a woman for him to argue with. She wore a floor-length robe that somehow managed to be both homey and sexy, comfortable but designed to hug the rolling curves of her body with the male eye in mind.

He sipped his can of Pepsi from the hallway machine.

"I'm feeling a whole lot better," he admitted. "Only now I'm beginning to think more."

He hadn't told her yet about what had happened. "Things can't be that bad. Where did Keith take you?"

"To a dead-end street—almost. How was the party after I left? Really boring, I'll bet?'

Her laughter was like music.

"I missed you a little bit," she admitted. "The room seemed so empty without you and your ego."

"Keep track of our other playmates?"

"Uh, I was hoping you'd forget to ask." Her breasts lifted beneath the robe as she drew in a long breath and sighed. "Okay, let's take them one by one. Who was where when you left?"

Madison rested his head against the back of the couch and squinted at the ceiling as if looking back in time.

"Jeremy and Laura were at the end of the serving table," he said. "I'd been with Brocchi. Mick was with you and the record reps."

"Ah yes, horny Mick," said Connie. "He might be interesting if I liked them fast and a little crazy." Madison caught her eye and grinned.

"But you're more the Taurus type, is that it?'

"Whoa, big fella." She grinned right back at him.

"Is this business or are you putting the moves on me?"

"Let's take business first and then see what happens. How did things go with Mick?'

"He might have gotten obnoxious except that Lee

joined up right after you left. I guess that inhibited Mick somewhat. He kept looking but at least I didn't feel like I was in danger of being raped at any second."

"How about Jeremy and Laura?"

Connie's face clouded with a frown.

"It was hard keeping very close tabs on them," she said. "I had my hands full with Lee and Mick. But from where I stood it looked like the two of them were arguing about something, and they weren't being too cool about it. They weren't shouting exactly, but you could tell things were heated. Then Jeremy turned and left her there and I had to bust my butt to get out of there after him without looking like an obvious fool."

"How long was that after I left?"

"Not long. Not even a minute, I'd say."

"Do you think Jeremy saw me leave?"

"I couldn't tell. Like I said, I had my hands full. It was a big party."

"And then?"

"You sound like an old Coasters record," she laughed. Then she sighed. "And then—nothing. I followed Jeremy through the lobby and over to the elevators. He seemed pissed about something. Anyway, he wasn't looking behind him. He caught the elevator and I went over and watched the dial. He got off on his own floor. The car came down and it was empty. So, I went back, to the party... and Lee and Mick were gone."

"They didn't waste much time," said Madison. "Jeremy splitting like that could have been just a diversion so they'd have a clear exit."

"But that's assuming they felt it was worth the work," said Connie. "Plus, Jeremy didn't have any contact with them after you left to set it up." Madison finished his Pepsi.

"I wonder just how smart those guys are," he said half to Connie and half to himself.

"So, let's hear about your adventures," she said. "Something about a dead-end street?"

He stood and walked to the window, looking down at his reflection in the glass and the lights beyond.

"A girl was murdered, and I was supposed to take the fall," he said tiredly. "They tried to tie drugs in with it and really hang my ass. Only a cop took too long pounding at a door and I got lucky."

Briefly, he told her what had happened after he left the party. By the time he reached the part about waking up with the blonde girl's corpse, Connie's face was drawn, and her fingers were touching her throat in a reaction of pure horror.

"My God! It doesn't seem possible..."

He turned to face her.

"Of course, it's possible," he said brusquely. "That's what I was trying to tell you on the plane. We're not trying to nail someone who snatches cookies from girl scouts. We're after someone who kills people. It doesn't bother the bastard at all, you'd better understand that. And he'll damn well kill again if he thinks it'll buy him anything."

"I remember the girl Keith was with when he left," Connie said slowly. "Was she the one?'

Madison nodded. His mouth was a hard line.

"Beautiful, wasn't she?" he said.

Connie didn't answer at first. Then her eyes brightened with a sudden thought.

"Then if Keith and Lee were talking to each other at the front door of her house," she said, "it must have been Mick who clubbed you!"

"Or Jeremy," said Madison. "It all depends on whether he was drawing you out of that party on purpose for Lee and Mick to cut out."

"They'd also have to know why you're really on the tour for that," she pointed out. "And they'd have to know that I was working with you."

"Whoever was playing that game, they'll be damned surprised to see me on the tour again tomorrow morning," growled Madison. "They'll try to stop me again. Only next time they might not play it so cute."

Connie rose from the couch and crossed to stand before him. The lights from outside illuminated the worry in her soft eyes.

"Steve, it isn't right for you to put your life on the block like this—"

"It's what Arn pays me for, Connie. Do you think he pays me ten grand just for insulting him?"

"But tonight...maybe if you'd stayed and explained to the police—"

"He doesn't pay me to get his name blasted all over the papers, either. He pays me to take care of business —my way. Hell, it's the only way I know."

Her eyes searched deeply into his. "Who do *you* think slugged you, Steve?' she asked.

"It's too early to tell," said Madison. "It also depends on how you want to figure it. I'd like to know how deeply Lee Brocchi is involved in things."

"I don't understand how he could show up at that girl's house," said Connie, shaking her head. "You would've been long gone following Keith by the time Lee and Mick were able to slip out of the party."

"There are ways," said Madison. "I seem to remember that a bunch of girls came into the party together. Maybe some of them knew the blonde girl. Maybe Brocchi or Adamson had time to get her address while you were following Jeremy. That's the only way it adds up right now. If Brocchi's on the level, he had a good enough reason for going through the trouble. I lit some fires under him just before I followed Keith out. Maybe he thought he was doing Keith a favor."

"If that's the case," said Connie, "where does that leave Mick?'

"That depends on whether he and Lee left the party together," said Madison. "Do you know for a fact that they did?"

Connie nodded.

"That's what Laura told me," she said. "I spent some time with her after I found them gone—before I came back up here to stew."

Laura. The hurt washed over Madison again for a moment, pulling at his stomach, but he tried to keep it from showing. Sweet Laura. *Sweet cheat...* "What did she say?' he asked blankly.

"Just that they walked out together." Connie paused as if debating whether to speak her mind. Then she said, "Most of our conversation was about you."

The way she said it made Madison forget about the hurt.

"Comparing notes?" he prodded, his eyes glinting.

"I didn't know there were notes to compare."

"And if there were?'

"I—I don't know..."

"Okay. It's only fair that you know what you're working with. Laura and I were very close to each other once. A long time ago. Very B.J.—Before Jeremy."

"So much for my powers of perception," said Connie. "I missed that completely. I thought I was getting to know her and the easiest way seemed to be to talk about men. I guess I was too bummed out about blowing my assignment to read the signals."

"You didn't blow anything. They were too slick or too lucky. It happened. Don't knock yourself out about it."

"What I am knocking myself out about is a question Laura asked me," she said. "At the time I thought she was just making conversation, and I didn't feel bad about not having an answer. Now...I don't know. Maybe I'd like to know the answer myself."

"Must have been a tricky question."

"I don't think so. She asked me what you and I meant to each other."

"Lady," she said, "that can be one of the trickiest questions in the world between two people: Especially on a rock 'n roll tour. Especially doing the job we're trying to do."

She turned from him, looking down into the street.

"It wasn't fair of me to pin you down like that," she said contritely. "I'm sorry."

He stepped behind her, moving his body against hers. The natural scent of her hair was like musky perfume in his nostrils. He slipped his arms around her. She showed no resistance.

"What would you like us to mean to each other?" he asked softly.

"I'm not sure," she said. "It wasn't a fair question. We're supposed to be doing a job. The only reason we're here together is that we both work for Arn. I tried to tell myself that tonight while I sat up worrying about you."

Madison turned her around. She was beautiful there, framed by the dark window and the mellow reflection of the city lights that stretched out like a bed of diamonds beneath her. An aura of sexuality emanated from her, igniting his whole system with a warm glow.

Sex with this woman would not be give and take, but an ultimate *sharing* of sensation and fulfillment. "Maybe we just need to step back from it for a while," he said. "Sometimes you can become so much a part of it, you forget who you are and what you need."

"I need to be a woman," she said simply. It was

almost a whisper. "I need to know that there's at least one other person in the world tonight who isn't like all the others I've met today. I guess I'd like to know that there's some love left in the world tonight." The sensuous lower lip extended in an enticing smile. "Or a little loving..."

"It's what we both need," said Madison.

He stooped and scooped her behind the knees and suddenly she was up in his arms, the house-robe billowing out beneath her. Her arms wrapped around his neck, her warm face drawing close to his. Their mouths met in an urgent, hungry kiss that was still working as Madison started toward the bedroom.

7

MADISON AWOKE WITH A START FROM DEEP SLEEP. HE was in a cold sweat. Someone was pounding on a door; wouldn't stop. For a fraction of time he was back on the hard, wooden floor of a nameless girl's bedroom, staring into dead eyes.

He sat up, shaking the disorientation from his head. Sunlight filled the room. The air was warm and muggy. He was in bed. Right. Connie Frazer's bed. Their love-making of the night before had been passionate, inventive and thoroughly exhausting.

That's why the sleep had been so deep. Connie's body was warm against his beneath the twisted sheets. She nuzzled in closer against him and purred.

But the knocking at the door wouldn't go away and the purr became a feline growl.

"My God, it can't be past six o'clock. Who could that be and why aren't they in bed?"

Madison grunted. Nude, he threw back the sheets

and got to his feet. He padded over to the window, parted the curtains and looked out. It was wet and dreary in Chicago, the sky a horrible off-gray color. And hot. He swore, jabbed the air conditioner unit into life and climbed into his slacks.

Connie had buried her head under a pillow. Madison appraised the lady's flowing curves, fully visible through the clinging sheets, with a fond, bitter-sweet glance. Then he left the bedroom and walked barefoot to the front door. He yanked the door open angrily.

It was Lee Brocchi.

"Let's you and I have a talk, Madison," he said without preamble. "I just got off the phone with Shapiro. I had the bastard against the wall and he finally leveled with me."

"Yeah, I was wondering if he would," growled Madison. He stepped aside and nodded into the living room. "Okay, but let's make it fast. The less people who know you're here, the better." He walked over to the open bedroom door, grabbed the knob and started to close it. Beyond Brocchi's line of vision, Connie Frazer had managed to prop herself up on her elbows, the sheets drawn around her breasts. She opened her mouth to speak. Madison shot her a cold glare and the words died stillborn. He pretended to close the door but did not bother to latch it. Turning to Brocchi he said, "It didn't take you long to find which bed I was in."

"I get paid to keep an eye on things," growled Brocchi. "With you and Connie I figured if it hadn't happened yet, it wouldn't take long."

Madison thought he heard a faint indignant gasp from within the bedroom, but he kept a straight face.

"We can talk, she's in the tub," he said. "Don't worry about her, she's just cover. Dumb."

"Yeah, Shapiro told me that too." Brocchi's mouth was a tight line. "I don't like crap like this being pulled behind my back. I'm running this tour. I could blow this whole crazy pipe dream of yours sky high if I wanted to."

"Relax," Madison told him. "We had to see how good you were. You tumbled—so you're in. So now that you're in, what do you think?"

"I think it's the biggest load of crap I've ever seen shoveled," said Brocchi, He was keeping his voice down only with visible effort. His words were a breathy snarl. "I've been through plenty with Jeremy. Me and the dude are like *that*. And now you're asking me to buy that he's a *vampire*—some psycho who gets his kicks killing with his teeth? I don't think so."

"Arn didn't accuse Jeremy of anything to you," said Madison. "We don't know who it is. What do you think the chances are that it could be Mick or Keith?'

"Christ! listen to what's going down," rasped Brocchi. "I'm rappin' on dudes I'm supposed to be working with!"

"If you're sure it's not Jeremy—" said Madison, and he let the sentence dangle.

"That's just as crazy," said Brocchi. "Those two

might be a little off the wall when it comes to all that occult crap, but don't forget it's earning them a few million dollars. I don't call that crazy."

"Somebody's killing somebody," said Madison. "Arn didn't make that up."

"The bastard was real generous with me," Brocchi told him, a dash of self-pity eroding the tone of toughness. "He appealed to my sense of morality and justice to help apprehend a killer if there was one on the tour, or he advised me that I'd be blacklisted out of the business!"

"Mick and Keith aren't your buddies," Madison reminded him coolly. "Last night at the party you told me that this was just a bread-and-butter gig." Brocchi's eyes narrowed. "You're really down on those two, aren't you?" Madison stepped back and rested against the arm of a chair. He was trying to read into the depths of Brocchi's eyes, beneath the words, and he was coming up with nothing. The tour honcho would be sudden death at a poker table.

"Where were you last night, Lee?'

"You know damn well where I was," snapped Brocchi. "You left me at the party when you took off after Keith."

"And you left a few minutes later. You and Mick."

Brocchi glanced at the bedroom door.

"She's the one who told you that. I thought you said she wasn't in on this?'

"She doesn't have to be in on it to keep track of people for me," said Madison. "That's why she's along.

So, what did you and Mick do with yourselves alter you left?"

Brocchi didn't bat an eye.

"We found a place up the street and had some drinks. We've all been partying pretty hearty since this tour kicked off. Mick felt like mellowing out and that sounded like a good idea at the time so I tagged along." He bristled. "Why? Am I on the suspect list too? Arn didn't get around to telling me that part."

Madison ignored the question.

"If just goes to show how wrong a guy can be," he said philosophically. "The way you were heating up when I cut out after Keith last night, I figured the first thing you'd do would be to find a phone and call Arn. Or follow me."

Brocchi's eyes were twin points of steel.

"I tried to reach Arn from the first bar we hit," he replied with no trace of emotion. "I couldn't get through until this morning. He had Led Zepplin playing the Garden and you know Shapiro when the stars are in town."

"But hell, Lee, I was walking out after one of your charges. You call that body guarding?"

"I saw the chick Keith had with him and I knew damn well that he didn't want a chaperone," said Brocchi. He cocked his head slightly. "What about you? I haven't seen Keith yet today? What happened? Does he know you followed him?"

"I didn't follow him." Madison lied blandly. "My driver was a real ace. We lost your boy before we'd gone two blocks. So, you and Mick spent the night getting quietly blitzed, in a neighborhood tavern, is that it?"

"That's it, yeah."

"What did you talk about?'

Brocchi's body seemed to tighten like an over-wound watch. He stepped forward, his knuckles white.

"You know, Madison, I've got a real suspicious idea that I'm being used here. And I don't like it worth a damn!"

He was going to say more but was interrupted as the bedroom door opened.

Both men turned as Connie Frazer entered the living room. She was dressed in Levis and a bright blue blouse. While it may have been humid in Chicago, the lady was looking cool and fresh. She'd come awake in a hurry.

When she picked up the vibes in the room she stopped, then started to turn.

"Oh...I didn't know I was interrupting a business conference," she said good-naturedly. "Sorry."

Madison rose from the chair arm.

"Just monkey business," he grinned. He turned back to Brocchi. "I guess that about ties things up for a while then, right, Lee?'

Brocchi started to say something in anger but again caught himself. He executed an almost military about-face and stiff-legged it across to the front door. He yanked it open and stood with his hand on the knob.

His eyes locked with Madison's. His poker face was back in place.

"I'm still thinking things over," he said. "I told Shapiro that I'd keep my mouth shut and help you out with this thing. Now I'm starting to think the wrong people are getting the help. If you're planning to railroad somebody just to keep Shapiro's skirts clean—"

"You know better than that, Lee."

"I'm still thinking it over," Brocchi repeated.

He slammed the door and was gone.

The room was heavy with silence. Madison broke the hiatus with a heavy sigh not unlike that of a golfer who's just sunk a particularly difficult hole- in-one. He looked back at Connie.

"Good work," he grinned. "If you'd stayed in there much longer he'd have thought you were listening."

She crossed to the armchair and half sat and half fell into it. Madison returned to its arm where he'd been sitting. He let his fingertips glide along the back of her neck. She purred just as she had in bed and reached up to entwine her fingers through his stroking ones. Her touch was electric. Then she remembered a thought and looked up at him.

"I don't understand why Lee told you he was with Mick last night, when you saw him at the house where that girl was killed," she said. "Or why you didn't call him on it when you knew he was lying."

"I think I know one of the reasons he lied," said Madison. "But people can do things for more than one motive. I need to do some more checking today."

The warm feminine fingers slipped away from his own.

"So, we're back to cryptic word games," she said. "Couldn't last night at least change *that*? Or is trust too much of a commitment to ask?"

Madison didn't stop stroking her smooth neck. "I trusted you enough to want you to hear that whole conversation just now, didn't I?'

"Yes, and that's something else I don't understand. What was the scam about Brocchi not knowing that I was listening in? If he's supposed to be working with us—"

"If he has any reason to, he'll see a chance to play us against each other," said Madison. "If he wants that chance, let's give it to him."

That broke the ice. She laughed despite herself. Her gentle fingers returned to his.

"You are a Machiavellian bastard," she said. "Do you think Lee knows about what happened to you last night? Was he part of it?"

"I don't know. If he was trying to set me up, maybe we can trick him into playing it so cagey that he'll foul himself up and save us the trouble."

"But maybe he was just looking out for Keith like he says."

Madison grinned.

"In which case, why should I put myself at the scene of a murder?"

"So, if we hypothesize that Lee doesn't know anything about the murder last night," said Connie, "we also hypothesize that Keith wasn't involved in what happened to you either. Lee and Keith were together for at least awhile after they split." Her brow knit into a frown. "It would have to be like that. We aren't talking about very much time. That means that it was either Mick or Jeremy who killed that girl."

The phone rang. Madison grimaced.

"That'll be Arn," he said.

It was.

"I see you're doing a real good job out there, Steve."

The voice dripped with sarcasm. Madison did his best to ignore it.

"You don't know the half of it," he said. "Someone tried to hang a frame on me last night. There's been another killing in the market."

Shapiro's explosion of breath sounded like a gunshot over the long-distance connection.

"Damn!"

"Yeah. It's nothing we can talk about on the phone."

"Was it...just like the others?'

"No," said Madison, "and that's what bothers me. Or maybe the whole number was just improvised on the spot and that accounts for it. I was supposed to take the fall, but it was too loose."

"For Chrissake, Steve, no one told you to join the tour and blow everything to hell! I just got off the phone with Brocchi about a half hour ago and he didn't say anything about...this new one. Does he know?"

"Uh-uh. Now it's my turn to ad-lib and I'm keeping him in the dark for a while."

"Is there any way what happened last night can come home to roost?"

"Don't worry, Arn. I covered my tracks."

Shapiro snorted. "At least you're starting to look after things in *my* interest for a change like you're being paid to do!" Madison chuckled into the mouthpiece.

"Or maybe I'm just waiting to get the guy in my own sights," he needled. "Anything I felt about the bastard before goes double now. Now it's personal. Our psycho tried to cook me last night, and I don't like that."

"What's the number with Brocchi?" the promoter asked. "You don't think he had anything to do with those...jobs?"

"The limos are leaving in about forty minutes, Arn," said Madison. "And I'm still in my birthday suit, more or less. You wouldn't want me to miss that flight to K.C., would you? I'll get back to you when things start happening."

Shapiro didn't think that was funny.

"You stay on the line, goddammit!" he bellowed from New York. "You don't need any forty minutes to get dressed. And what do you mean 'when things start happening'? I'd say too damn many things have happened already!"

Madison's grin grew wider.

"Now you're the one who's starting to come around," he said. "That's what I've been telling you all along." He pushed the disconnect button with his index finger. When he released it the dial tone buzzed in his ear. He dialed the desk. "If I get any more calls, I'm not to be disturbed," he said. "Under *any* circumstances."

He waited for the smart "yes, sir!" from the operator, then hung up. Once again, he seemed to glow with satisfaction. But Connie Frazer had been listening to the one-sided conversation with mounting perplexity and concern.

"I think you just aced yourself out of a job," she said, "and I don't know whether to feel sad or relieved."

"Consider it academic," said Madison. "I doubt if Arn will even bother trying to call back."

She worried her lower lip and shook her head as she appraised him unabashedly.

"I don't know, Steve. Sometimes I think you're too damn sure of yourself. It'll catch up with you someday."

Madison stalked over and stood facing her straight on in the chair.

"Maybe you should learn the name of the game we're playing," he said evenly. "It's called playing both ends against the middle. That's what I'm doing with the guys in the band and that's what Arn is playing with us. You heard what Brocchi told me. Arn made him think that you weren't working on this with me. Now why do you think he did that?"

Connie was staring at him like something under a microscope.

"You guys *are* scary when you start playing games," she said quietly, again in awe but with none of the good humor of before.

"Don't throw ethics at me," Madison told her. "You're taking a cut and you knew what you were getting into. You can bow out anytime you want if the job's too much for you."

"I'll be able to handle it, thanks," she bristled. "I guess the scheming side of you was just one I hadn't seen before. It'll take some getting used to."

"It's just another way I earn my pay," said Madison. "And while you're getting used to it, you can start thinking about Brocchi and how you're going to handle him if he does decide to play us against each other. Because you're the one he'll go to."

"What about you?" she asked.

Madison's grin slipped back into place. Morning always was his best time.

"Me, I've had enough wheeling and dealing for a while," he grinned. He leaned forward and delivered a chaste kiss to her forehead which failed to register any response whatsoever. This didn't seem to faze him in the least. He straightened and started toward the bedroom. "I should just have time for a quick shower," he said. "Then we'd better get down to the loading zone. I've got a feeling Brocchi isn't going to look around too goddamn hard for us if we're not there when the cars pull out!"

8

If you're a rock star, there is a form of fatigue which hits at about mid-point on tour that is like no other. For nearly two weeks now your life has been the hotel and motel rooms, the limos, the airplanes, constant movement. Always something to do, something happening, someone around. Many, many someones. It's a transient existence. There is no place, nothing, to call your own. Your world is a numbing flow of sensation and experience seemingly without beginning or end. It's up at nine or earlier and you're rushed to the airport. Then the flight to the next city on the tour. Just enough time to check into your room —plastic, aseptic, void of any personality whatsoever, just like all the others— then down to the sight of the gig for a sound check. Lots of "hurry up and wait." There's some hanging out with musicians in the group who will be sharing the bill with you but there's little to say. They're as burned out as you are. Back to the hotel or motel for a fast dinner. Nothing but ill-prepared commercial grease that fills the stomach but could never be said to nourish. You might have time for an interview or two, then you're climbing into your stage clothes and the road manager is at the door every thirty seconds reminding you how late it's getting; that the limo is downstairs waiting to whisk you back downtown to do your show and earn your money. After the show there's the ubiquitous party tossed by the promoter or record reps to give themselves a chance to hobnob with the stars. You're in bed by two or three at the earliest and tomorrow at nine or earlier it starts all over again: another city, another gig and more partying.

It was fun at first, sure. The realization of every true rocker's dream: playing your music for fun and plenty of profit and living the nomadic life of a gypsy, with all the women, dope and booze you can handle tossed in to make it complete. Until the days and the cities and the faces all merge into one repetitious blur. The pot and dope have kept you going until now, giving everything around you a stoned glow that at least made it all-easy to experience and enjoy. But by now you've indulged in so very much in such a short time, with so much happening, that it's all caught up with you. By this point the pot and drugs only anesthetize, leaving you spent, foggy and irritable.

You wish it would stop. Or even just slow down. You wish you could get away by yourself for just an hour, thirty minutes would do, to enjoy the almost forgotten beauty of solitude and silence. Man does not live by energy alone. But it doesn't stop. There are another fourteen cities to go on the tour. And the madness—the constant assault on your senses—continues around the clock. Day after day after day.

The show goes on.

That's where everyone's head at on The Screaming Tree tour this day as the Learjet soared through sunny skies at 32,000 feet, well above the clouds. It was still raining below, but here the world was a crisp blue beyond the cabin portals, although everyone in the plane seemed too wasted to take notice.

Steve Madison had experienced mid-tour fatigue often enough to recognize its symptoms in others. Each one of his traveling companions had it bad. Or seemed to. Mick Adamson, Lee Brocchi, Jeremy Bates and Connie Frazer inhabited a semi-circular couch up front toward the pilot's compartment.

They were watching a video Cassette of an old *In Concert* T.V. segment with blank, barely comprehending eyes.

Laura Bates sat a few seats behind them at a window seat across the aisle from Madison. A half-finished paperback book was spread open across one of her shapely knees. Her head was resting on a pillow propped between the seat and the wall, and she appeared to be dozing.

Keith Terrance was beyond a paneled wall to the rear of the craft. There was a well-stocked bar back there and some couches. But Terrance would be alone.

Madison was as quiet as the others. He sat gazing out through the window beside his seat. This was only his second day on the tour and, though he had been through a lot during the last twenty-four hours, he was a long way from being victimized by the fatigue which had these others in its grip. He was keeping a low-profile, blending in with the surroundings so as to be hardly noticed by these people in their sleepwalking haze. By tonight they'd begin coming to life again. But this was only late morning. Dead time for any musician worth his salt who'd been working as hard as these guys.

For Madison this was a time to get things done. For Connie too. Despite appearances she wasn't any more wasted than he was. She was following his instructions, hanging out with Lee, Mick and Jeremy around the cassette machine to try and pick up any bits and pieces of the puzzle which might happen to float her way. She hadn't said much to Madison since their stretched tempers that morning. But she was working with him, helping him, getting the job done,

Madison wondered if he was bothering her mind as much as she was bothering his. He liked her the more he thought about her, and he'd been thinking about her a lot since the lift-off from O'Hare. He blocked her from his mind once again, determined that this time she would stay blocked out. He brought his thoughts back to the matter at hand.

Tonight would be interesting. There was no concert scheduled for this evening. The band had the night off in Kansas City before playing a show the following evening across the river at Mun Stadium in Independence. Tonight, everyone would have their first free time since the tour began.

It would be interesting to see what they did with it.

Madison folded that morning's edition of the *Chicago Tribune* which rested on the seat beside him and pushed himself lazily to his feet. With paper in hand he ambled down the aisle toward the bar beyond the partition. No one seemed to notice his leaving.

Keith Terrance was situated behind the small bar in the process of fixing himself a gin and tonic. The hefty drummer glanced up as Madison slid onto the stool across from him. An oversized hardbound book was open on the bar top, pages up. Madison lifted it to read the spine. *The Satanic Bible* appeared in gilt lettering.

Madison set the book down.

"Looking for new song material?' he asked.

"Just reading," said Terrance. "Name your poison, promo man. This one's on the house for the pushing around I gave you in the dressing room last night."

This was the first time Madison and Terrance had confronted each other since the backstage ruckus at Soldier Field the night before.

Madison's expression was unfriendly.

"I remember it the other way around, Keith," he said. "You're the one who took the knocks, remember? Give me a soda."

Absolutely no reaction registered on the drummer's broad face. He reached beneath the bar, came out with a bottle and popped open the top. He set it before Madison alongside a glass. Madison ignored the glass. He took a long pull from the bottle. When he set it down he realized that Terrance was staring at him. Still no reaction.

"You don't think much of getting along with people, do you, Madison?"

There was a trace of accusation to the question.

"I told you last night, I just don't think much of prima donnas," said Madison. "You want to forget what happened last night? Okay, we'll forget it. But let's keep the facts straight. I'd hate to have to refresh your memory with another demonstration."

When the reaction finally came it was without warning.

Terrance's arm flashed with a speed that belied his size and the bottle of Pepsi flew from the bar, thumping loudly against the opposite wall. Terrance's face twisted into something ugly.

"I'm tired of trying to get along with you, bastard," he snarled. "Seems to me like you're the one with a chip on your shoulder. Who the hell do you think you are, turkey? I take bastards like you apart for exercise!"

"Save it for the mirror," said Madison.

He opened the copy of the *Tribune* to an inside page and slid it across the bar between them until the edge of the paper crinkled against Terrance's bearlike chest. Terrance glanced down irritably—and seemed to go on

Holiday. His eyes narrowed in on the small article which Madison had previously circled in red.

"What is this?" he growled.

Madison's voice was cold and even as he asked, "Care to tell me where you went last night after the party, Keith?"

Terrance reread the address in the article, then looked back up. There was some new emotion flickering way back in his eyes, but Madison wasn't sure what it was.

"You followed me," the drummer said dully. "What is this, a shakedown?'

"That girl the article is about, the one who was murdered," said Madison. "Was she a pickup, Keith? Did you meet her last night or had you known her before?'

"I've got a better question," growled Terrance. "Why should I tell you? What were you following me for? What the hell are you doing on this tour anyway? You're no promo man. I smell a cop, and that's the worst kind of smell."

"That's three questions," said Madison, "and you're a little slow. Brocchi decided I wasn't a promo man last night."

"Yeah, he told me, but I wasn't sure," said Terrance. "I suppose you saw him at that chick's house last night too?"

"I saw him."

"Then you know that he hauled me out of there and that the girl was alive when we left. She saw us to the front door. Lee kept his taxi waiting while he went in and got me."

"Maybe I didn't see everything," said Madison, emphasizing the last word.

Terrance nodded, his hands knotting into ham-like fists on the bar.

"Lee was right," he said. "A lousy narc on the make. Only things didn't work out and now you're trying to hang a frame on someone else, is that it?"

"Maybe you'd better explain that, Keith."

"Explain, hell! What happened, man? Did you go in to have a talk with her after you saw Lee and me take off? She was a nice piece. I oughta know.

Maybe you like your work too much. Some cops are like that. Maybe things got out of hand."

Madison kept his surprise to himself. Keith Terrance possessed a quick mind beneath that Cro-Magnon skull. The drummer had ad-libbed a perfectly plausible interpretation of the physical evidence at the scene of last night's murder.

"That's good, Keith. But I wasn't responsible for that girl's death, and if it means anything, I don't think you were either."

The drummer's eyes grew speculative. The hands were still fists.

"Who do you think did kill her?' he asked. "Someone on this tour?"

"I don't know," Madison replied truthfully. "But I'm going to find out. And you don't have to worry, Keith. Lee was just flying off the handle when he showed up and dragged you out of there last night. Mrs. Madison didn't raise any narcs. I'm into copping a buzz as much as anyone on this plane."

"So, who are you, man?'

"Let's just call me an interested party."

"Uh-huh," said Terrance.

There was nothing even closely resembling trust in the response. Madison decided the hell with it and moved on to a new subject.

"Jeremy tells me that you and Mick write the lyrics for the band's songs," he said. "He says all of the occult stuff comes from the two of you."

"*I* write the lyrics," said Terrance. "Sometimes when I'm stuck for a word, Mick will help out. But it's my material. Those are my lyrics."

"I get the picture," said Madison. "You write the lyrics. But you don't really buy all that Satanic crap, do you?"

Terrance didn't take offense.

"I take what I want from it."

"Like what? I'd really like to know."

As if he were onstage, the drummer didn't miss a beat.

"Like the knowledge that I'm a complex being with a full set of emotions," he said. "When they bury me, when my time comes I want to go knowing that I've *lived!* That I've experienced each of my emotions and passions to the fullest. That I haven't short-changed myself. That's why they were given to me. Labels like *good and bad* have been invented by spiritual eunuchs who don't have the guts to live on the edge, at the height of their passions. What I've learned from my studies of the occult and the teachings of Lucifer has freed me from sharing their fear. Baudelaire once wrote—"

The guy showed no sign of slowing down. "Spare me the quotes," interrupted Madison. "That sounds more like Leopold and Loeb than Baudelaire anyway, and you know what happened to those two wingdings. That trip only takes you one place, Keith. Up against someone a little heavier who thinks the same way. Or against someone who might just decide to take you out of the picture on general principles."

"It's been tried," said Terrance evenly.

"That girl last night wasn't the first woman to drop dead on a Screaming Tree concert tour," said Madison. "How far would you go for thrills, Keith? Would you go to the point of taking a human life? How sick are you?"

Terrance didn't answer the question directly.

"I was loaded when you took me in the dressing room last night," he said. "I'm straight now. I think you need to be taught a lesson, Madison. Carving my initials in your face is one sensation that should be a real pleasure!"

The articulate spokesman disappeared, and the Cro-Magnon man was back. He didn't waste any more time on words. He didn't waste any more time, period. He came around the bar. He reached into a pocket, producing a small object in his fist. He flicked it and a seven-inch blade seemed to appear from nowhere, the blade glinting evilly.

He started forward in a low crouch.

Madison's reaction was immediate and instinctual. His hand dipped beneath the left lapel of his jacket. When the hand reappeared, it held the .44 Magnum, hammer back.

Keith's momentum carried him forward until he was halted by the muzzle of the gun pressing against the center of his sloping forehead. Then he froze, not moving a muscle. Tense, knowing how close he was to death. The knife dropped.

The only sound in the small lounge was the constant dull humming of the jet engines through the craft's shell. They seemed louder now.

Keith was still in his crouch, but his arms had spread even wider apart, away from his body to indicate submission. The paleness of his face resembled the underbelly of a fish.

"Whoa—" He was working hard to keep from shaking and only half succeeding. "Put that thing away, man! I was only rough housing..."

The moment held like that. A frozen sliver of time. The smell of fear was thick in the room.

Finally, Madison stepped back, easing down the Mag's hammer but keeping the drummer covered. He slowly backed up toward the archway leading back into the passenger compartment. His unblinking eyes had all the life of crushed ice. But he was reading the drummer and there was no mistake.

Terrance knew how close he'd been to joining his beloved Lucifer, for sure.

But the drummer was also animal enough to sense that he was to survive this confrontation. Carefully, he stooped and retrieved his knife, folding and pocketing it.

"Why don't we try it one more time and play fair," he suggested. "I put up the sticker, you put away the heat." His huge fingers were clenching. "I want to take you apart *bad*, Madison."

"Who the hell said anything about playing," Madison told him. "This is work, Keith. All work."

"You never did say what your work was," Terrance reminded him, his self-assurance returning by the second. "If you're not a narc...what are you?" Madison's eyes grew cold.

"I could be an avenging angel," he said with no trace of humor. "I've come for someone on this tour, Keith. If you did have anything to do with that girl's death last night, get your affairs in order."

Terrance opened his mouth to say something, but at that moment Lee Brocchi stepped through the archway. Something in the atmosphere of the room tipped Brocchi off immediately that things weren't right even before he saw the gun in Madison's hand. He saw something in Terrance's expression. Then his gaze shifted, and he did see the gun. He uttered a gasp of surprise and darted a hand toward the left lapel of his own jacket.

Madison flicked the Mag back to *Safety* and holstered it.

"Relax, Lee. I was just showing Keith a few gun tricks. Quick draw stuff."

Terrance was enough of a performer not to miss his cue. All the tension seemed to flood from his animal-like body and he returned to behind the bar like a gracious inn keeper.

"What can I fix for you, Lee? How about you, Madison?"

"Thanks, but I'll sit this one out," said Madison. He brushed by Brocchi and passed through the archway back into the cabin proper. Brocchi followed him and caught his arm in a tight grip just beyond the archway. The others were still up front, lost in their video cassette.

Brocchi's face was tight with rage.

"What the hell was going on back there?" he snarled. "I'll be damned if I'll stand by while you—"

Madison yanked his arm free.

"You're damned already for putting up with that line of jive for as long as you have," he said. "By the way, why did you lie to me about where you went last night?'

"You mean after I left the party? Why should I lie about that? I was out drinking with Mick, like I told you."

"That's not the way Keith tells it," said Madison. "He says you trailed *him* out to the near North Side of Chicago last night. He says you pulled his ass of some girl's bed because you thought I was a narc or some similarly undesirable type, out to make a bust."

As he listened, Brocchi's anger seemed to dissipate. It was replaced by wariness.

"Why don't we go back and talk this over with Keith?" he suggested.

"You talk it over with him," said Madison. "I find the guy a bore. And since you are going back in, ask him to show you the article I circled in today's *Drib*. It's on the bar. I think you'll find it real interesting reading."

He turned his back on the road manager and returned to his window seat, across and two back from Laura Bates who still seemed to be dozing.

As he gazed once again out into the endless blue and listened once more solely to the high keening whistle of the craft's engines, the trace of a smile curved his lips. Keeping things stirred up, yeah. Keep everybody on their toes. The *status quo* was that there was no *status quo*.

Someone would show their hand before the band left Kansas City. Madison had his eye on all of them, waiting for the break. Waiting for the sign.

And just keep stirring...

Next on the list was The Screaming Tree's lead vocalist and bassist, Mick Adamson. Madison's smile soured to a grimace as he remembered the passionate clinch that Mick had gone into with Laura the night before in the Chicago-hotel parking lot. He suddenly realized with a reapproving shock that he'd been putting off confronting Mick because of what he'd want to do to the bastard. Laura was another man's woman by marriage. Madison was willing to recognize that and expected other men to do the same.

Madison diverted his mental flow from carrying that line of thought any further. Keep the emotions out of it, Madison. When the emotions flame up and take over, some of the other senses dull. This is a killer you're trying to nail. His next victim could be you.

The gang up front by the video machine had replaced *In Concert* with *Star Trek* and seemed to slowly be coming to life. Connie managed to glance back and meet Madison's glance. The connect held just long enough for Madison to know that she was on the job. Then her attention moved back to the show. Beside her, Jeremy Bates was slumped down as if he didn't give a damn about the space opera on the machine, but that there was nothing better to do so he was stuck. Beside him, wiry, compact Mick Adamson was a study in contrast, hunched forward off the couch, his full attention riveted on the video drama, oblivious to everything else.

It would hardly do to question him now in front of the others. So, Madison spent the remainder of the flight reviewing and trying to make sense out of what had happened. The conversation with Terrance was a puzzler. It suggested a hell of a lot more questions than it answered.

When Madison had told Keith that the girl last night wasn't the first woman to drop dead on a Screaming Tree tour, Terrence hadn't even questioned him about what he meant. As if Terrance was damn well aware of the string of murders that had trailed the band across the globe.

And Arn Shapiro had thought he was the only one who'd figured out the connection.

Was Keith Terrance as astute as Arn Shapiro?

Or was Terrance a psycho who liked to rip open women's bare throats and revel in their blood? Was *that* how he knew what Madison was talking about?

Someone was going to tip their hand in Kansas City. Madison was willing to bet on it. And yeah, it could be Terrance.

There was only one reason why Madison had told Terrance that he didn't suspect Keith of the girl's murder in Chicago last night. If the drummer thought that he was not under suspicion, he would relax and that would give Madison more room to swing in this investigation. And Madison had a feeling he could use all the breathing space he'd be able to get. Things could get very tight, very quickly. In addition, if Terrance wasn't the psycho, he might even try to lend a hand and dig something up on whoever was doing the slaughtering.

Madison hadn't even been thinking of that angle when he'd originally gone back with the *Chicago Tribune* to confront the drummer, and now his smile returned as he decided that, despite some of the new questions it had raised, it had been a satisfactory conversation overall after all.

Yes sir, he was doing a fine job of scrambling these people's minds.

Application of the final touch came only after they had landed in Kansas City.

Madison knew K.C. to be an old, ugly town, but none of that was apparent from the airport. They had left the storm pattern. The midday sun beamed down a refreshing, warm glow, a happy change from the raunchy mugginess of Chicago. A breeze was blowing as they debarked the plane and walked toward the two waiting limos, and as the breeze ruffled his hair, Madison experienced a thankful gladness to be at least this far west. Another eight hundred miles and he'd be home in Colorado.

Ever-smiling Jeremy Bates and his Laura and Connie Frazer started for one of the cars, Jeremy and Connie avidly discussing the shows which Laura had napped through. Madison fell in behind them.

Keith, Mick and Brocchi were climbing into the other caddy. But at the last minute, Keith detached himself from them and caught up with Madison, as Madison, the last one to his car, was just about to climb in.

Brocchi leaned out from the first limo. "Hey, Keith! I thought you were riding with us. We're all tired, man. Let's go!"

Terrance ignored him. He looked at Madison and spoke with his voice low, dangerous.

"I still want to know why you followed me to that

girl's house last night," he growled. "Tell me why you followed me. Now."

Brocchi's voice called again from the other car. "Come on, Keith! Let's roll."

Madison nodded toward the road manager.

"I don't know what you and he spent the rest of the flight talking about," he said to Terrance. "But he's the man to fill you in on that angle."

The drummer's face clouded. "Lee?"

"I didn't follow you last night," said Madison, as if it were a statement of obvious fact. "I made all that up. Lee's the one who told me that you were at the scene of a murder. He followed you, just like he said. When I leaned on him this morning, he couldn't stop singing. He's got a real good voice, that boy has. You ought to try using him in the group." He slid into the car the rest of the way and slammed the door in Keith's face. "You heard Mr. Brocchi," he snapped at the chauffer who was furnished by the limo service. "Let's roll this popsicle wagon."

The machine slid effortlessly into gear and left Terrance standing in the sunlight. Madison's caddy swung around toward the access road leading to the highway. He had one last view of the hulking drummer as Keith turned slowly and marched back to where Adamson and Brocchi sat waiting in the first limo.

Madison thought it was a shame that he couldn't make out the look on Keith Terrance's face.

He didn't envy Lee Brocchi one damn bit.

9

IT WAS A DAY OF SURPRISES FOR MADISON. FIRST, TO learn how lucid Keith Terrance could become relevant to matters of satanism and the occult. Then, that it would not be at all difficult to arrange a confrontation with the next name on his list.

He received a phone call from Mick Adamson within minutes after checking into his motel room.

Kansas City was as gloomy and dilapidated as Madison had remembered it, even in the sparkling summer sunshine. This had once been a swinging, wide open town in the days of bootleg whiskey, a young Count Basie and Kansas City jazz. *With my Kansas City baby and my bottle of Kansas City wine.* Sure. The music lived on but the happy-go- lucky red-light spirit that had given birth to it had died long ago, smothered by the sterility of countless moral "clean up" campaigns.

Or maybe he was being too hard on the place.

Maybe it was just his mood. Knowing how short the fuse was getting. Wishing for but a passing instant that he could remain here in the plastic but at least safe comfort of the Holiday Inn room. Leaving the problems of the world—especially Arn Shapiro's problems —to take care of themselves. He thought again, as he occasionally did on assignment, how paradoxical it was that he had to smear himself with the dirt and moral decay of others, to pay for his retreat out among the healthy, soulful virgin pines of the Rockies. Or maybe it wasn't a paradox. Maybe he learned something here —about himself and the universe he lived in, its good and its bad— that gave the golden peace of his time away even more meaning.

He turned from the window and started toward the door. Connie Frazer was two rooms down. He wanted to learn if she had picked up anything hanging out with Lee, Mick and Jeremy around the video machine in the plane.

He had his hand on the knob when the peeling ring of the telephone pulled him around. He hesitated an instant. There was a good chance it would be Arn Shapiro calling from New York, trying to keep tabs on him.

He briefly debated with himself the and advisability of just letting it ring and going on about his business. But somehow Shapiro always seemed to find a way of tracking him down, and there seemed little use in prolonging the inevitable. He walked back to the phone and lifted the receiver.

It was not Shapiro.

"Let's you and me have some words," a voice said. It was Mick Adamson.

"Talk on, Mick. I'm all ears."

"Not over the house phone," the lead singer snapped peevishly. "I'll meet you in the coffee shop next door. Not the motel coffee shop. I don't want to run into anybody. I mean the one about halfway down the block."

"No one booked me in as a secret agent," Madison replied. 'What's wrong, Mick? You know what room I'm in. Drop on down and let's have a talk."

"I'll be at a back table," said Adamson. "Be there in fifteen minutes."

The line went dead.

Twenty minutes later, Steve Madison strolled into the coffee shop. The place wasn't crowded, and the Screaming Tree's lead singer was easily spotted, even at a back table. The wiry, compact singer and bassist seemed even more antsy than usual. He was flying, either on something synthetic or on the quivering of his, own stretched nerves.

"What the hell's the idea of keeping me waiting?" he demanded irritably as Madison slid in across from him. "You were supposed to be here five minutes ago."

"What's five minutes?" said Madison. "I was across the street. I watched you come in. I wanted to see if anyone was playing tag with you."

"Was there?"

There was a quaver to the voice now. The eyes said

he was flying on a chemical high. But the quaver said that the nerves were jumpy as well. Madison wondered what he'd hooked onto here.

"There was no one following you," he said confidently. "Relax."

Then the waitress was there to take their order. When she had gone, Adamson said, "Something's going down on this tour that I don't know about. I want that to change."

"Why come to me?"

"Because I think you're right smack in the middle of it, that's why. What did you say to Keith back there by your limo just after we'd landed?" Madison shook his head.

"That's between Keith and myself," he said.

"And *that's* what I'm talking about," rasped the singer. "This band was never what you'd call family to each other, the way a good band ought to be. Sure, I'll admit it. Between Keith and me, Keith is the heavy. I listen to what he says because a lot of it makes sense. But it's not a fifty-fifty exchange and we both know damn well that the only reason I'm around is because when I sing his lyrics, people buy the records and we both get rich. Then there's Jeremy, putting Keith's lyrics to music for as long as the paychecks keep coming. And Lee's head is right where Jeremy's is at."

Madison nodded. "A real mixed bag of nuts," he agreed.

"But at least we got high and had some fun with

each other," the singer snapped. "At least we trusted each other."

Madison couldn't hold back the words that came next.

"You've got your nerve, talking about trust," he growled. "Screwing your lead guitarist's wife."

Adamson's rubbery lips seemed to quiver with a life of their own as Mick drew in a quick breath. He licked his lips and most of the quivering stopped.

"I knew that had something to do with it," he said. "Does Jeremy know?"

Madison ignored the question. "Tell me what happened in your limo after I spoke with Keith," he said._

Mick shrugged and spoke impatiently, as if he considered this the price for getting on with more important matters.

"When Keith got back into the car with me and Brocchi, he seemed really pissed," he said. "No one said anything for a little while but after we'd gone a ways, Keith says to Brocchi, "Madison tells me maybe we should fit you into the group." Brocchi didn't seem to know what he was talking about, so Keith goes on, "Madison says you told him all about what happened at that chick's house in Chicago last night."

Madison grinned to himself. It made him feel good to know that his efforts were meeting with success. He said, "And Brocchi told Keith to stow it until they were alone. Or words to that effect, right?"

The singer started. "How did you know?"

"You said something about being mad because no one trusts you," Madison reminded him.

The food arrived.

And with the food, another interruption.

Lee Brocchi and Keith Terrance came leisurely in through the front door. Brocchi spotted Madison and the singer and the surprise was clear on his face even from across the room. Brocchi and Terrance conferred for a moment, then came forward. They both seemed in good spirits.

Adamson muttered a graphic curse. He leaned forward and Madison leaned over to listen. He had the impression that the singer was flipping as rapidly as possible through his mental index file of sights and geography assimilated in the short time since they'd arrived in town.

"Look, I've got to talk with you and I want to do it where we won't be overheard," he said. "I don't know what highway we came in on, but we passed a big gravel quarry just after leaving the airport."

"I remember the one," said Madison.

"Good. Meet me there tonight at nine. It could be worth your while."

"Yeah," said Madison dryly. "We can talk all about trust."

Then Brocchi and Terrance were with them, joining them at the table. It seemed that they were in dire need of sustenance, but that they had had to bypass the Holiday Inn coffee shop since Keith had a supreme distrust of any food made in any chain kitchen anywhere.

Madison admitted to sharing this prejudice and he and Adamson dug in while Brocchi and the heavy-set drummer ordered meals of their own. The conversation drifted to the state of popular music today, and during it Madison could detect no undercurrent of distrust or bad vibes between any of th men around him. It was hardly a personal discussion, but the words flowed easily, seemingly between friends who enjoyed each other's company. Any hostile undercurrents were successfully muted beneath the pleasantries.

Madison made a point of finishing his lunch and being on his way before any of the others. He didn't want to be tied down by a group. He wanted to have the freedom of movement without needing to explain anything to anybody. Besides, he wasn't picking anything up or accomplishing anything hanging out here discussing who was on top of the charts this week. If any of these guys had anything to say about the events of the past few hours, they were waiting for him to split before they said them.

So, he split. With smiles and see-you-laters, he paid his check and walked back toward the motel up the block. He had been about to see Connie when Adamson's call had come, and now seemed like as good a time as any to follow through with that original plan. Besides, he was looking forward to seeing her again, alone, even if it was just to compare notes on the assignment.

He walked a little faster.

The lady was getting under his skin...

Which was why, when he saw Jeremy Bates helping Connie into a rental car in the motel parking lot, he suddenly felt the same vast emptiness in the pit of his stomach that he had felt the night before when he'd seen sweet-cheat Laura go into her clinch with trusting buddy Mick Adamson in Chicago.

Connie and The Screaming Tree's lead guitarist didn't see Madison. From this distance, their manner seemed to be that of a man and woman who were friends, out to share a pleasant afternoon drive in a new city.

The car pulled away and exited the lot on the opposite side of the block, immediately lost in the dense flow of traffic on the street which ran parallel to the one on which Madison stood.

He tried telling himself that there was nothing to worry about. Connie must have picked up a lead on the. plane. Like a good operative, she was following through. Madison hoped the lady knew what the hell she was doing. But there was no possible chance of catching up with them now...

He continued toward the motel. The emptiness he'd felt at seeing Connie and Jeremy together was still there. Only it wasn't like last night in Chicago after all. Seeing Laura with a man other than her husband had brought disillusionment. There could be no disillusionment with Connie. Madison had no illusions about her. There hadn't been time since yesterday morning in New York to form any.

A lot more had gone by in those twenty-four hours than a few thousand air miles. There was a spark between himself and this woman; a compatibility. And thanks to an extraordinary set of circumstances, their lives had intertwined as totally as their bodies had the night before in Connie's bed.

Madison recalled that just before the concert last night at Soldier Field, Connie had told him that she and Jeremy Bates had once been lovers. The thought had somehow been lost until now beneath the flood of everything else that was happening. But now it registered, and Madison was surprised at the realization that this time the emptiness in his gut was jealousy, and nothing else. He reminded himself that he had no right to be jealous of a woman he'd only slept with once.

Then he found himself wondering why it wasn't Laura Bates out driving with her husband.

He found Laura in the motel cocktail bar.

There were only two other customers in the place, and she was sitting alone at the bar. Madison had always felt that bar stools enhanced the appearance of some women, while others, no matter how virtuous, had trouble getting comfortable on the damn things without giving the vague impression of being tramps. But a lady was a lady anywhere and that was how he had to class Laura Bates, even after what he knew about her.

He slid onto the stool next to hers.

"Buy you a drink?'

"No th—" she started to say. Then, when she realized who it was, "Oh! Steve—"

Madison looked at the bartender.

"A Coors for me and another of whatever the lady's having," he instructed. Then he looked back at Laura. "I never remembered you as killing your spare time in cocktail lounges, lady."

She looked at him directly for the first time. There was something deep in those brown eyes that he couldn't be certain of. There was a time when he could read her like a book. But that was long ago. He sensed an air of unhappiness about her, though, and wondered how to handle it.

The drinks came.

When the bartender was out of ear shot, she said, "I thought we agreed last night to stay away from each other. Not to mess up each other's life all over again."

Without knowing why, he asked, "Any idea where Jeremy is right now?"

Her eyes grew sharper.

"No. Why?"

Madison took a sip of beer and shrugged.

"Just wanted to check up on when I should arrange this interview that some local columnist's been pestering me for," he said. "I am the promo man, you know."

She sipped her drink, a Marguerita, eyeing him over the glass.

"I guess I'm still trying to get used to that," she said. "I guess I always saw you as so much more."

"It's kind of late for the personal jabs, isn't it, Laura? They say first you love, then you hurt, then you forgive. I thought we were way past the second stage by now."

She turned back to the bar with her drink. The air of tragedy—or maybe it was just sadness—that he'd detected before was even more pronounced.

"We are past that stage," she said. "I'm sorry. I didn't mean to hurt. I guess I meant that since we split, I've always thought of you as playing your music, being happy." She tried to smile but didn't quite make it. "I guess that's just my hang-up, isn't it?"

His thoughts of Connie Frazer were obliterated in the presence of this woman who had meant so much to him. As were any thoughts of cheats, sweet or otherwise. A part of hm wanted now so badly to reach out to her. But he knew he couldn't do that.

"I guess I always thought of you as being happy after we split up too," he said. "It doesn't look like either one of us got their wish, does it?"

She looked at him. She seemed to be genuinely startled by the statement.

"What do you mean, Steve?'

"*Are* you happy, Laura?"

"Steve, please—"

"Maybe I'm just misreading the signs."

"Signs?'

"Like you and Jeremy arguing at the party last night, for starters."

"Stephen don't be silly. Jeremy and I are married, remember? Married people are supposed to bicker once in a while."

"The next day you're sitting down here drowning your blues in Margueritas while your old man's seeing the sights with another lady?" Madison countered. "Yeah, a real happy relationship the two of you have. And I've only been around for one day."

Laura's brown eyes blazed. | "That's right, only one day," she said. "So, what the hell gives you the right to try and diagnose my entire life after only one day, just because we knew each other a long time ago? I've been living and growing since we broke up, Steve. I might not even be the same person you knew way back then."

"Two years isn't that long," said Madison. "What were you arguing about last night? Did I cause it?" She shook her head. Madison thought that her long brown hair glinted beautifully in the soft lights of the lounge.

"You're more impossibly stubborn than you were two years ago," she said. "No, I told you last night that Jeremy doesn't know about us. You remember the mutual agreement I told you about? My past stays buried where it belongs, in the past, and so does his." She set her glass down. She reached along the edge of the bar and touched his wrist. "Dear Stephen, we can't let the past confuse us about what's happening now. Don't you understand that? There's a part of my heart which will always belong to you, and I know that a part of you is loving me right now. You want to help me, but you don't know how to go about it because you have no way of knowing what kind of person I am now. You can't help me, Steve. Please, just let it be. You'll save us both so much hurt."

It was quite a speech. When it was over Madison finished his beer and got to his feet, dropping some dollar bills on the bar.

"You always were impossible to argue with, yourself," he grinned. "You're much too logical for a woman, Laura. Okay, I'll lighten up. Your life is your life. And so are your problems. I'm sorry."

"Thank you, Stephen."

"Take care, lady."

He caught the elevator in the lobby and all the way back up to his floor he wondered what had happened down there. He flashed back on his condemnation of and pontificating to Mick Adamson less than thirty minutes ago and tried not to feel like too much of a hypocrite. But dammit! There *was* still some sort of magical flow between himself and that fine woman. It could never be as it once was, obviously. He had blown that long ago. But a feeling was still there. Then he stopped thinking about it.

In his room he locked and chained the front door. It was three-thirty in the afternoon. He stripped and took a fire-breathing, twenty-minute shower. He didn't bother toweling down as he padded out from the bathroom. He liked the sensation of the moisture evaporating from his skin. Nude, he sat at the narrow shelf built into the wall beneath the mirror and cleaned and oiled his .44 Magnum.

As he worked over the powerful weapon, he thought about his scheduled meeting with Mick Adamson for nine that evening at the gravel quarry. Of course, it could be a trap. It was only last night that someone had snuffed another human being simply to frame him from the picture. Maybe tonight they were going for the direct approach. If that were the case, the setup would have to be damn near airtight before Adamson would put his neck on the line by luring Madison out there. The singer would have to feel certain that Madison wouldn't walk away alive.

Which was all the more reason to go, if forcing people's hands was the name of the game.

If it wasn't a trap then maybe, as the singer had hinted, Madison would learn something from Mick that he could use. Although Mick had seemed far more interested in learning facts than in divulging them.

With his cleaning chores completed, Madison carried the .44 back to bed with him, setting it within easy reach on the pillow beside his head. He set his alarm clock for eight o'clock, just in case, and flicked on the T.V.

He fell asleep midway through a rerun of *I Love Lucy that* he'd seen twice before.

10

THE SIGN READ: SLOAN GRAVEL COMPANY.

The area was bordered by a high chain-link fence. Beyond the fence the interior was bathed in the faint silver glow of a three-quarter moon. The hulking outlines of parked heavy-duty dump trucks took on a vaguely sinister air. The conical shapes of mini-mountains of gravel were like ghostly pyramids, pointing their tips at the clear dark sky. Two heavy padlocks held the front gates securely shut, supposedly without effort. He dropped to the opposite side with a muffled *thump*.

It was precisely nine o'clock.

Traffic was light on Route One-Sixty-Nine, just a few hundred yards behind him. Occasionally the full-throated roar of a semi rose above that of the cars. But those sounds, and the occasional hum of a jet overhead on its way to or from nearby Fairfax Mun Airport, were the only reminders to the lone man in the darkness that was surrounded by a metropolitan area. The light at the foot of those gravel pyramids was solitary, silent and uninviting.

Madison strolled forward along the dirt road which led on to run between the gravel heaps. His footsteps seemed to echo. He reached beneath his jacket and checked the looseness of the Magnum within his shoulder holster.

He wondered where Adamson was.

The alarm clock had brought him awake an hour earlier. He'd ducked under the shower again, only a fast reviver this time, and had quickly dressed and made his way out here in a hotel-furnished rental car.

The car was parked at the shoulder a half mile away. Madison had been early. He'd kept an eye on the front gate of the place for close to twenty minutes. A quick reconnoiter before stashing the car had ascertained that the front entrance was the only entrance. But no one had showed. So, Madison was the first one there unless they had been waiting since before dusk, and that didn't seem likely. People who plan to kill people try to avoid the sunlight.

Madison had entered the grounds 99 percent certain that he was alone on them—but still cautious.

If this wasn't a trap, he had a feeling that he knew what The Screaming Tree's lead singer was so anxious to talk about.

When Madison had first asked Brocchi where the road manager had been after the night of the girl's murder in Chicago, Brocchi had answered that he'd been out drinking with Adamson. Madison knew this was untrue, and he suspected that Adamson had asked Brocchi to alibi him. He'd have a damn good reason as he was spending the late-night hours with his band mate's wife. Now that Mick was aware that Madison knew the truth of his whereabouts on the murder night, he'd naturally be afraid that Madison might tell Jeremy. He would be coming here tonight to talk Madison out of any such action.

Madison had a little polite blackmail in mind. He still wasn't sure how deeply Brocchi was involved in setting him up for that girl's murder in Chicago. Mick had been hanging around a lot lately with Brocchi, and maybe, through accident or design, he'd picked up something that Madison could use to determine Brocchi's guilt or innocence in the matter. And with what he knew about Adamson and Laura, he figured he'd have enough of a lever to make the singer sing. It would be his price for keeping silent about Adamson's betrayal of a friend's trust. An image of Jeremy Bates driving off with Connie Frazer flashed across Madison's mind. He didn't owe the guitarist a thing!

So here he was. Still trying to solve a murder. Still hot on the vampire chase. Standing in the dark. Waiting for something to happen.

Waiting alone.

Madison's body was more loose-jointed than usual, his knees slightly bent. Every battle sense, never lost since the jungle days of Nam, was finely honed to detect any movement whatsoever from the shadows.

There were none.

It was as if he were alone in the world.

He got tired of waiting.

"Mick!" he called. "It's me, Madison!"

The rising roar came suddenly from the direction of the highway behind him, beyond the fence. It had begun as a rumbling part of the traffic flow, but had suddenly burst from the pack, gears shifting expertly as the roar rose still further to a rapidly gaining white hot scream.

Madison spun—and was blinded. He stumbled back, one arm lifting to shield his eyes while the other hand darted beneath the jacket to his shoulder holster and came out with the Magnum on full cock with the safety off. Ready to blast.

The truck roared down on him.

The deafening howl of the engine and the height of the headlamps told him what to expect. Probably a Mack Truck. One of those, twenty-five-ton dump truck jobs. Thirteen gears, two sticks. A monster. The screaming truck barreled up the access road that led from the highway. It plowed through the front gates at full throttle, tossing aside the links of metal like the unwanted toys of a temperamental child."

Madison hadn't hesitated through indecision. The truck driver knew his shit. He'd catch any attempt to dodge and still squash Madison like a bug. But he might be so sure that Madison was stunned by the powerful lights that a move at the last possible instant could do the trick.

At the last second Madison jumped sideways, hitting the ground with his shoulder and rolling, propelling himself from the path of the monster. Madison came out of the roll and onto his feet. He could taste the settling dust. The .44 was up, fanning the darkness.

A hundred yards away the driver of the truck was still working the complicated gear shift. The rolling, mountainous shadow never slowed down. It swung in a wide circle, powerful headlamps slashing the dust-clouded darkness. Then it came back at him again.

This time he was ready. He stood squarely in the full glare of the approaching lights, aiming the Magnum in a classic shooter's crouch, left hand bracing the shooting wrist.

He had one wild impression of being trapped in a tunnel with a powerful express train barreling down on him and nowhere to run.

Then he fired.

He picked off the right headlight and the monster became a cyclopsed. But he had misjudged. The truck was coming down on him faster than he had calculated. Its engine was screaming. And once again he was on the thinly wired edge between living and oblivion, with only reflexes to decide his fate.

He leaped again, this time to the other side, behind the lower reaches of one of the gravel pyramids. The driver caught the move this time. But in reacting, he over-reacted. He tugged on the wheel too hard, cutting in too sharply onto the pile of gravel. The front tires began climbing the slope long before they could get anywhere near Madison. The driver spun the wheel and corrected his mistake. The cyclops gunned out down the road a stretch. Then it swung around again. The single spotlight caught Madison and held him, and the monster came forward for the final death charge.

Madison crouched. He took a two-handed aim again. But not at the remaining light. The Magnum boomed in his fist. It was echoed by the fainter explosion of the truck's bursting right front tire.

The bastard had nine other wheels, but the front hit slowed him down. The truck began to wobble horribly in the moonlight.

Madison straightened.

There was hurried movement from the darkness to his left.

A form materialized before him, charging. A long, slashing steel blade glinted in the darkness, ripping downward at him,

Madison twisted to receive the attack. His upper body swung free from the path of the descending blade. His hands grasped the wrist below the knife hand and twisted brutally until the knife dropped. His right leg straightened, and his foot neatly tripped the attacker and sent him spinning.

Madison's vision was still pin-dotted from having stared into the truck's headlight. He couldn't make out any physical characteristics of his attacker. He was barely able to make out the shadowy form, or to see what it was doing.

Without warning, the form's hands grabbed his ankles and yanked, releasing and pushing at the same time. Madison tumbled onto his back on the rough pebbled ground. Somehow the Magnum went skittering from his fingers.

Now his vision was returning. Now, as he looked up and saw the still shadowy figure of his attacker. The figure was stretching its arms above its head. And the arms supported an enormous jagged rock. With a grunt, the figure began pitching the jagged edge toward Madison's head on the downswing.

The rock never connected.

A gunshot echoed amidst the pyramids. The sound of a ricochet. The rock sailed backward from the shadow's grasp, away from Madison.

The shadow lashed out with its foot. The foot connected with Madison's jaw, sent him reeling away again. Madison landed on his hands and knees. He thought he saw his gun laying a few feet ahead of him in the moonlight. Or maybe it was three guns.

"Get the hell out of here!" a voice shouted warningly. "Trouble!"

A truck door slammed somewhere in the distance. And the slapping sounds of two pairs of retreating feet drifted to him. His vision was still blurred from the vicious kick, but at least the three Magnums that had been swimming before his eyes a moment ago had now solidified into one. He grasped the butt and his finger slid around the trigger. He was on his feet, literally angry enough to kill.

New footsteps approached from his right. Feminine footsteps. He lowered the .44 hammer; held his fire.

Connie Frazer approached him in the moonlight.

She was dressed in white slacks and a light- colored blouse that rode with the up-down sway of her full breasts as she approached. Quite a woman...and looking mint julep cool despite the short-barreled .38 she carried at her side.

Madison looked off in the direction from which he had last heard the retreating footsteps. Apparently they were abandoning the truck. Maybe it even belonged here. But in any case, they would have a car waiting somewhere in the vicinity as a precaution. By now they had enough of a head start to make pursuit a waste of energy.

He looked back at Connie.

"I thought you were down on the law of the gun," he said. "You shoot like Annie Oakley."

"It comes from going for a summer with a guy who was a police cadet," she explained. "He was always dragging me to the firing range. But don't slow down to thank me for saving your life. I know how busy you are."

"That is one I owe you," he admitted. "Anytime you need me, Connie, anywhere you are, just holler. I'll save your life as many times as it needs it. By the way. How did you get here?"

"I was coming in one entrance of the lobby back at the motel while you were going out the other," she said. l called after you, but you were so intent on something that you didn't even hear me. I figured that anything that had you that occupied must be important. So, I thought I'd tag along and see what was up."

"You mean you were watching the whole time that homicidal crazy was trying to run me down with a truck?"

She nodded.

"I was betting on the truck for a while," she said. "So where do we go from here? Do you have any idea who was driving it? Or who his friend with the knife was."

"No," said Madison. "But I know who set me up for them." He rammed the .44 into the shoulder holster angrily. He grabbed Connie's hand that wasn't holding the .38. "Come on," he said. "Let's go calling. Now it's my turn to dish out some lumps."

They took off toward their parked cars at a dead run.

Connie said nothing on the ride back into town. She had parked closest to the quarry, so they took her car,

Madison wasn't worrying about how he'd get his car back. There were other things on his mind right now. His hands gripped the wheel, the knuckles white, as he tooled in and out of the traffic flow, eyes staring straight ahead. His face was a set mask of silent, powerful rage. The gas pedal stayed close to the floor all the way back to the motel.

11

MADISON WHEELED THE RENTAL CAR INTO THE HOLIDAY Inn parking lot and screeched to a stop, peeling rubber, amid the out-of-state cars and the vacationers stretching their legs while one of their party registered at the front desk. He left the car, moving at a brisk, stiff-legged pace through the lobby's front entrance.

Connie Frazer jumped out after him without bothering to slam the car door behind her. She hurried to catch up with him.

His grim singularity of purpose was already turning heads in the lobby. More heads turned as the stunning blonde reached his side. They passed through the doorway leading to the stairwell together. His long legs took the stairs two, sometimes three, at a time. With effort, she kept up. The .38 was now residing in her purse.

"Steve, maybe you should cool off before talking to anybody," she said. They had just passed the fourth floor and were still climbing fast. She was beginning to lose her breath. "Maybe they'll be waiting for you."

Madison didn't slow down.

"That's fine with me," he said. "I'm looking for a fight. I don't like being set up like a clay pigeon in a shooting gallery."

Then they reached the musicians' floor. Madison slammed through the stairwell doorway and stalked directly to the room that was shared by Mick Adamson and Keith Terrance. Connie came up beside him as he tried the knob. The door was locked. He pounded on it fiercely.

It was opened a moment later by Keith Terrance. The heavyset drummer was barefoot, dressed in faded blue jeans and a white T-shirt. A television blared in the room behind him.

His manner wasn't surly, but he didn't seem to have much interest either.

"Yeah, what is it, Madison?"

"I'm looking for Mick," said Madison.

"Then you'll have to look somewhere else. I haven't seen him since about three this afternoon."

"I'd like to check for myself, thanks."

Terrance started to say something in protest. But Madison was already brushing by him. A fifteen second search proved that the drummer had been telling the truth. The singer wasn't on deck. Madison turned and stalked past Terrance, back into the hallway.

Something in Madison's manner had warned

Terrance to keep himself in check. As Madison and Connie next moved down to Lee Brocchi's room, the drummer followed.

Madison repeated his routine, pounding on the door. The door was yanked open irritably by the stocky road manager. He appeared to have been napping. He squinted like a man who's been yanked from a sound sleep.

His glance took in the three people before him, then centered on Madison.

"What the hell do you want?" he seethed. "The first time I've been able to slow down enough to take a nap in what seems like twelve years, and you—"

"I want Mick," snarled Madison. "Right now. Where is he?"

"How the hell should I know?" snarled Brocchi right back. He was coming awake in a hurry. "I haven't seen the dude since this afternoon."

"You're forgetting what you told me this morning in Chicago," Madison told him. "You're paid to keep an eye on things, remember? And you strike me as a guy who takes a lot of pride in a job well done." Madison kicked the door open the rest of the way. He shoved Brocchi with two powerful hands and stepped into the room as the road manager stumbled backwards. "Now tell me where that little turkey is," he demanded. "I don't have a helluva lot of time."

Brocchi caught himself, then held his ground. He eyed Madison for a moment, then looked beyond him at Keith and Connie, who had also entered the room. His head snapped in the direction of the doorway.

"Both of you, split," he said. "This is just between the two of us."

"Connie stays," said Madison. "A few things have changed since the last time we spoke, Lee." Brocchi didn't pause to consider.

"Okay," he said. "Keith, beat it."

Now, finally, anger did rise within the drummer. He started toward Brocchi.

"Now wait a minute, Lee. I don't like being talked to that way—".

As he passed, Madison reached out and grabbed Terrance's arm above the elbow in a steel-like vise.

"Aren't two rounds enough, Keith?" he asked. "I'd think you'd get tired of waltzing with me. Why don't we just do this one very mellow? This is Lee's room. Let's do like he asks, okay?"

He released the drummer. Terrance stood there unmoving at first, rubbing his arm. He stared from one to the other of the three faces before him. Then he turned toward the door.

"Fuck the bunch of you," he growled. "I was just getting down with some good T.V. when this bastard started coming on heavy."

He was still grumbling as he slammed the door behind him on his way out.

Brocchi shot Madison a tight grin.

"It looks like you've mastered the art of handling

Keith," he said. "Just call his bluff." The grin went away. He nodded toward Connie but was still looking at Madison. "This morning you told me she was just along for cover. Shapiro told me the same. Is that one of the changes you were talking about?" Madison nodded.

"One of them," he said. "Connie just pulled my ass out of the fire, and I figure that ought to be worth something. So, from now on she's in. Now where the hell is Mick? Shacked up with Laura Bates again?" The road manager flinched.

"You know about that?'

"Don't sidestep the question, Lee. I don't want to lose the mad-on I've got for that boy. Where is he?" Brocchi was still side-stepping. He emitted a sigh that must have come from his ankles. He seemed determined to justify himself.

"I guess I was a fool to think it would stay under cover as long as it has," he said. "I don't know if it happened on any of the other tours. But then Laura always seemed a lot happier in the past with Jeremy than she has this time. They've been squabbling a lot on this tour, and it hasn't all been the pressure of the road. It looks like a marriage going sour. Maybe Laura's just feeling low." He shook his head. "It's hard to figure her and a guy like Mick. But sometimes you can get so low, you just don't give a damn if you sink any lower. Yeah, I had the picture. But I figured it would be better to let it slide until the tour was over. Jeremy's my friend. I like to think my good friend. But this tour is business. People have to work out their personal trips on their own time."

"I guess you didn't hear me, Lee. I don't give a damn about any of that. Where are they?"

"Why do you want to know?'

"Someone just tried to kill me. I think Mick might have set me up."

Brocchi grabbed a coat that was slung over a nearby chair and slipped into it.

"They're in a motel out on the freeway," he said. "Part of the business agreement is that Arn has to be able to reach any of them within twenty-four hours. I'm the middle man. The band has to let me know where each of them is around the clock."

He stopped at a dresser near the door and pulled a .45 from the top drawer. He dropped the gun into the jacket pocket and led the way out of his apartment.

In the hallway, Madison looked at Connie. "Maybe you'd better stick around the motel here," he suggested, "I don't know where we'll end up tonight. You could be keeping your eyes and ears open."

Connie shook her head, just once.

"I'm going with you," she said. "I've earned my ticket on this ride. I'm the third *partner* now, remember?"

Brocchi looked at Madison.

"Ain't working for Arn Shapiro fun?' he asked rhetorically.

Then they were on their way.

Silence again reigned in the car as Madison sped across town. The only words spoken were Lee Brocchi giving him terse, monotone directions. Connie sat between the two men in the front seat. She stared ahead, worrying her full lower lip between strong white teeth. She held her handbag in her lap with both hands.

As Madison drove through the night, his mind was busy weighing and analyzing this sudden rush of recent developments. If Mick wasn't at this motel they were going to, that could be damning evidence that he had been involved in knowledgeably setting Madison up for a kill.

What should have been a thirty-minute drive was cut in half. The motel Mick and Laura had chosen for their evening assignation was not part of a chain. It was small and anonymous. Madison parked the car.

"They're upstairs," said Brocchi. "Number eighteen."

They had parked at the foot of the stairs leading up to the open balcony that provided access to the rooms. Madison led the way. Connie was behind him and Brocchi brought up the rear.

Madison reached the door of unit eighteen and knocked, hard. When that didn't bring any response, he pounded repeatedly with a closed fist.

Finally, the door opened, but only a few inches. Enough, though, to reveal the emaciated, rubber-lipped face of The Screaming Tree's lead singer. A taut chain stretched across the opening of the door, keeping it from opening any further.

Adamson appeared startled and a little angry at the sight of the three faces before him.

"Hey, what's going on? Lee, for Chrissake, have you lost your mind, bringing Madison and the chick here? You know who's here with me!"

Madison didn't give Brocchi a chance to answer. He said, "You and I had a date for tonight, Mick. Why weren't you there?"

"Don't try to get heavy with me," Adamson snarled from behind the security of the door. "Who says we had a meeting? What's this all about?"

"Steve says he was set up for a hit tonight," Brocchi told him. "He thinks you had something to do with it."

The singer's complexion—not very healthy to begin with—paled suddenly.

"Hey, now don't fly off the handle, man. I can explain!"

"Why weren't you there?" asked Madison. Adamson licked his lips.

"When I found out this afternoon that you knew about Laura and me, I figured I'd better talk to you alone and try to set things right," he said. "But when I told Laura that I was going to meet you, she flipped. She said that she'd talk to you. That she'd handle it herself. She begged me not to go. She... she's got a way of making me change my mind. I'm sorry I didn't show up. But I had nothing to do with setting you up to be killed, Madison. I swear it. I don't know who could have done that."

"You told me you had some information I could use."

"I know. But I was just saying that. I was afraid you

might not show up otherwise. I was gonna offer to pay you."

Madison's rage had cooled considerably since leaving the gravel quarry. But hearing that this little bastard had even considered that he might take a bribe to keep silent, now stoked the fires back to full blast. But he did his best to hold himself in check.

"Did you tell anyone besides Laura that you were supposed to meet me tonight?" he asked.

"No! No one. I don't understand how anyone could have found out!"

"Is Laura in there now?"

"Yeah, she's back in the bedroom. But you can't come in now! She's... we were just—"

"Open up, Mick." Madison's voice was cold and sharp. "Someone tried to nail me tonight and I plan to nail them back before their trail gets cold. If Laura told anyone that I was supposed to be put at that quarry...that's the sucker I want."

"So, talk to her in the morning," said Adamson. His voice held a-pleading tone. "At least let us get the hell out of this motel. Jesus, man—"

Madison stepped back and lifted a leg.

"Get out of the way, Mick," he warned.

He smashed a powerful foot forward. The door swung inward, pulling the chain brackets from the wall with a loud ripping sound.

He stalked into the room with Connie Frazer and Lee Brocchi still behind him. Brocchi's hand was sunk into the jacket pocket where he'd stashed the .45.

Adamson had heeded Madison's warning and stepped back. He was barefoot, dressed only in slacks and a halfway buttoned shirt which he had obviously just tossed on. He looked at Madison with wide eyes that seemed as wired as usual. He was outnumbered, but he didn't give up trying. He walked alongside Madison as Madison crossed briskly to the closed door in the opposite wall. The singer was frantically licking his lips.

"Now, have a little respect!" he was saying as they approached the bedroom door. He was trying to sound forceful, but it wasn't coming off at all. "You've got no right to come busting in here like this—"

But by then Madison had his hand on the bedroom doorknob and was swinging it inward.

He stepped into the room and stood for a moment —staring.

Adamson was right behind him. His gaze followed Madison's. The scream he gave then was almost feminine.

"Laura!"

Connie and Lee were right behind them. This time a feminine gasp really did fill the room.

"Oh—" cried Connie as she looked past Madison. Her eyes became wide circles of horror. *"My God..."*

Lee Brocchi made a noise from deep in this throat. Then he sighed.

"I'd better call the police," he said.

He turned and left the bedroom. Madison moved toward the bed.

Laura Bates lay stretched out on her back, nude, across the rumpled covers. But her slim, willowy loveliness was an obscenity now. She was dead. Madison touched her. She was still very warm. Her once-lovely face was twisted into a horrible, grotesque rictus of death. Her throat had been freshly slashed from ear to ear. Her blood still pumped rich and red from the gaping wound, wetly staining the bed sheets and dripping steadily onto the carpeted floor.

1 2

IN THE VERY EARLY DAYS OF HIS WORK FOR ARN SHAPIRO, Steve Madison had learned that rock stars were capable of getting themselves into all sorts of trouble. The very lifestyle of the big money rocker— the sudden fame, the temptations, the frustrations, the drugs—is ready-made for scandal and sudden death. The lifestyle hadn't changed at all since the pattern was set by people like Jimi and Janis and Mama Cass. And Elvis.

Madison's job depended on his capability at yanking the stars back out of trouble. His technique usually consisted of simply throwing himself full-tilt into the eye of the hurricane, as he had on this tour, and acting on instinct as a catalyst, until matters had resolved themselves to his employer's best interest. The nature of Madison's work being what it was, his trouble shooting assignments had taken him into several homicide investigations around the world. And while he had learned that the details of a police interrogation will differ from city to city, or from nation to nation, there is always one constant: the building inner heat of impatience that comes with having to endlessly repeat the same set of facts, over and over again.

That's the way it was now in Kansas City.

The police released Madison at eleven o'clock on the morning after Laura Bates' murder. He'd had his fill of talk. He wanted to get out on the streets and *do* something. He hadn't told the police about his former relationship with the dead woman; that they had once been close in all the ways people ever could be. But inside, that was all he could think about. The memory of his love for Laura, of her love for him, was a cherished thing. Her death would be avenged. But he had said nothing of those feelings during the last twelve hours of questioning. The police would be interested in that. They would get in the way of what he had to do.

The first thing the police had done upon arriving on the scene was to separate him from Brocchi, Adamson and Connie Frazer. He hadn't seen them since. He imagined that they had spent the past twelve hours much as he had.

Now they had told him he was free to go. He had stepped from the office where they were holding him— and had run into the other three in the outside corridor.

The twelve hours had done something to rub away

the New York cool of Connie Frazer's demeanor. She seemed weary, but more natural. Earthy. Her eyes met Madison's and flickered, but that was all.

Lee Brocchi just looked like someone in a hurry to get out of there. There was an almost awesome sense of silent rage about him. Madison knew that it must be the same impatience he himself was feeling.

Mick Adamson appeared to be in a hurry to be gone too. But there was nothing determined in his manner, as there was with Brocchi. Adamson looked like someone who was being startled by ghosts everywhere he looked.

They all seemed as surprised to see Madison as he was, seeing them.

"They just turned each of us loose too," said Brocchi.

He wasn't slowing down, but that suited Madison. He joined the parade toward the main exit at the end of the hallway, walking alongside the road manager.

"Did they let you talk to each other?" he asked Brocchi.

"Hell no," rasped Brocchi. "You know what they were doing as well as I do. Picking our brains to see if the stories fit together right. Keeping us separated so we wouldn't work anything up between us."

From behind them, Connie said, "Well, we must have done something right. They gave all of us a clean bill of health. They don't think any of us had anything to do with Laura's death."

"Or maybe they just don't have any proof," said Madison. "Maybe they're just waiting for one of us to trip up."

"Get ready," said Brocchi. "Here come the reporters."

The men of the media came at them through the doorway which they had intended to use. The reporters had been outside on the steps enjoying the sunshine, probably with one of their number keeping an eye on the corridor which ran past the interrogation rooms. That one had given them the high sign and now they all burst down on Madison's group at once, waving tape recorder microphones and spewing questions, each trying to be heard over all the others. A few live minicams bobbed around toward the back.

Since Mick Adamson was the lead singer of a popular rock group, most of the hurried questions were shouted at him.

"Mr. Adamson, do you have any comment?"

"Mr. Adamson, the police have only released the bulletin that they were questioning you about the murder of Laura Bates. They haven't released anything yet. Could you tell us what happened last night?"

"Mr. Adamson, was there any romantic link between you and Mrs. Bates?"

Adamson didn't answer. The foursome didn't slow down; They only tightened their ranks. Brocchi and Madison, in front, functioned as a human wedge, working ever closer toward the street entrance. The crowd of reporters moved with them, clustering in even closer to catch any chance remarks that might happen to be made.

Madison suddenly caught a new surge of activity from off to this right, beyond Brocchi. Some commotion beyond the heads of the reporters, working its way forward.

"Oh, shit," said Mick Adamson.

He said this as Jeremy Bates broke in through the inner circle of reporters.

The hulking form of Keith Terrance trailed in behind Bates, but Madison barely glanced at the drummer. His eyes were on Jeremy. The lines of the lead guitarist's once-good-natured face were now distorted with violent emotion.

Jeremy only had eyes for Mick. The scene in the hallway seemed to freeze for an instant, like a stop-time photograph, except for Jeremy making a beeline toward the wiry singer. Adamson tried to step back but was stopped by the throng.

"Jeremy, *no!*" he screamed.

"What were you doing in bed with Laura?" screamed Jeremy. His hands reached out for Adamson's throat. "What did you do to her? *You killed her*—"

Lee Brocchi came to life. He stepped forward, placating.

"Now slow down, Jeremy. Mick didn't—"

Jeremy showed no signs of slowing down or changing his mind, so Madison went into action. He stretched out his right foot and caught the guitarist neatly between the ankles moments before Jeremy's hands would have closed around Adamson's skinny neck. Jeremy went sprawling.

"Get him out of here," Mick was screaming. *"He's crazy!"*

The crowd of reporters fell back in the wake of violence. Jeremy was scrambling to get up on his feet. Madison stood before him, his legs spread, his arms loose and his fists barely knotted. Ready to knock the guy down again if necessary.

Then Keith Terrance was between them. His bulk towered over Jeremy Bates. He stood behind Jeremy. His arms circled Jeremy's chest, and he raised him to his feet. But he didn't let the guitarist go.

Bates was struggling to break free, trying to grab at Adamson.

"Let me at the bastard!" he snarled. "He killed my wife...he tried to kill Madison... he's no damn good! I'll kill him!"

In addition to holding him, Terrance was trying to bodily shake some sense into Bates.

"Jeremy! Jeremy, shut up, dammit! You're makin' a fool of yourself!"

Jeremy wasn't about to quiet down. He was still fighting to break loose, to get at Adamson. But Terrance was still holding tight.

Madison glanced at the reporters. They had regrouped from the sudden assault through their ranks. Tape recorders were running. The minicams were being lifted again. He looked back at Terrance and nodded curtly toward the street door.

"Get him out of here," he snapped. "now." Terrance obeyed, hauling Bates toward the exit.

"He was cool until we got down here," Terrance was saying. "We got here, and he just went nuts..."

"The best thing to do is split up," said Brocchi. He looked at Adamson. "Come on, Mick. We're taking the side way out. Let's *move!*"

The two of them split off in the opposite direction as Terrance and Bates, who had just disappeared through the exit. The reporters were already running around calling out loudly that wouldn't at least *someone* stay around and answer a few questions?

Madison felt a hand slip through his own. The fingers were long and warm. It was Connie Frazer. They were standing next to a stairwell and Connie was already holding the door open with her other hand.

They took the stairs down three floors to the street level, and none of the reporters even tried to follow them. They must have figured it would be better pickings with the stars.

They stepped into the sunshine and started down the wide stone steps toward the street. The warmth of the sunlight felt great after the hours of being questioned in a tight, stuffy office. Madison wondered briefly if the other two pairs of escapees had made it away safely.

He then became aware of the fact that Connie Frazer was leading him, ever so subtly, diagonally down the steps toward a car which stood waiting at the curb.

When they got there, Madison held the door open for her. It was a two door and she slid into the back. He sat in front and had barely closed the door before the car took off. He turned his attention to the man behind the wheel.

"Morning, Arn," he said conversationally. "Welcome to K.C."

Shapiro's ulcer was giving him trouble. Madison could tell by the way the nervous tic flinched around the dapper young promoter's right eye as he drove.

"You don't seem too surprised to see me," Shapiro snapped.

"I wasn't expecting you," said Madison. "But now that you're here it makes sense. The cops offered me one phone call after they picked me up. I turned them down. I imagine they extended the same offer to Connie." He looked back at the blonde woman. "She decided to make a collect call to New York and get the head office out here."

The lady didn't mistake his tone.

"We didn't seem to be doing very well on our own," she said evenly. "I had to save your life at the gravel quarry—only to have you drag us into a homicide investigation way on the other side of town."

She didn't say it as a nagging woman. It was delivered as a statement of fact, which Madison didn't dispute.

"Speaking of which," interrupted Shapiro, now

looking at Madison, "how about a report? The police haven't released a goddamn thing yet. That's why those news people came down on you so hard. All they had was that Jeremy's wife had been murdered and that one of the group was being held as a witness. Hell, that's all they even told Jeremy." He made a sour face. "As if that wasn't enough for the headlines!"

"I'm afraid there's going to be more," said Madison, and he reported to Shapiro what had happened between Jeremy Bates and Mick Adamson in the hallway of the police department. He finished with, "I'd say most of the stations and papers caught Jeremy's accusations. It didn't sound good." Shapiro could only shake his head. He drove staring blankly ahead for at least a minute. "And to think that I wanted you on this tour to keep things quiet," he said at last.

Madison tried to keep the irony from his voice. "If it does anything to help your ulcer, I kept quiet on the vampire angle," he said.

Connie Frazer's lovely smooth forehead creased with a frown.

"I'd been wondering about that," she said. "Do you think there's a tie up between this vampire psycho and Laura's murder?"

"I'm working on that assumption," said Madison. "Things have been happening too fast over the last two days for them to be unconnected."

"But what about the police? If they don't know anything about our original assignment, why are they letting everyone go? Since Laura was in bed with another man at the time of her murder, I'd think Jeremy would be the first one to be booked."

"Jeremy and Keith showed up in the cocktail lounge of the Holiday Inn around ten-thirty last night," said Shapiro. "Jeremy told me that when he and Keith briefed me at the airport this morning. The reason he's still walking around is that the police say it's stretching it a bit to imagine that he'd slash his own wife's throat across town, then race back to the Holiday Inn to sit down and have some drinks with Keith. He came unglued completely when he heard the news. He was a little more together when I saw him this morning. But then it looks like he came unglued all over again just a while ago, doesn't it?"

"Laura was murdered either just before or during the time that Lee, Connie and I were talking to Mick at that motel room," said Madison. "The way I understand it, neither Jeremy nor Keith have an alibi for the exact time of death, right? If the murder occurred about ten, either Keith or Jeremy *could* have done it and still showed up at that cocktail lounge by ten-thirty."

Shapiro's expression turned even more sour. "Sad but true," he admitted. "All Connie asked was why the police haven't booked Jeremy. They're not saying they won't, Connie. They're just saying that there are enough extenuating circumstances for them to look around a little more."

Connie nodded.

"I guess you were right," she said to Steve. "They're just waiting for someone to trip up, aren't they?"

"Just because they don't make a pinch doesn't mean they don't have suspicions," agreed Madison. "They just don't have any proof yet. We haven't heard the last of their questions, you can bet on that."

"Which reminds me," said Shapiro. "What about my question? Where's my report?"

"Where do you want me to start?" said Madison. "When Connie and I hooked up with this tour there had just been another vampire killing and our psycho must have been paranoid. Or maybe he sees it as being careful. Anyway, he put together who I was and what I was trying to do, and he's been out to nail my ass ever since."

"You weren't exactly keeping undercover," Connie reminded him.

"I'm not complaining," said Madison. "But the point is, they tried to frame me with the dead girl in Chicago, then they tried for me again at the gravel quarry. My guess is, Laura knew something and after the hit at the quarry fell through, they rushed over to that motel and slit her throat to keep her from naming any names."

"Isn't that kind of over-reacting?' asked Shapiro. "Not if she knew something that would put the killer away. Murder comes awful easy once you've already tried your hand at it. Especially when it looks like one more murder is all it will take to cover up the others. It's called kill-crazy."

"Who's this *they* you keep mentioning? I thought we were dealing with one guy?"

"There were two people trying to hit me at that

quarry," said Madison. "Someone drove the truck and he had a backup with a knife waiting in the wings in case anything went wrong." Briefly, he told Shapiro why he had gone to the quarry and what had happened there. Then he looked at Connie. "You were sitting with Mick and Jeremy around the video machine on the flight out from Chi," he said; "Pick anything up?"

"Only that this was the first time anyone on the tour has been to K.C.," she said. "But I guess that doesn't help much, does it?'

Shapiro didn't give Madison a chance to reply. He was still trying to get his facts straight as they pulled into the Holiday Inn parking lot.

"So, after you were attacked at the quarry, you came storming back to the motel where you figured everyone would be, and you got Brocchi to take you over for a confrontation with Adamson. Is that it?"

"That's it."

"Now for the biggie," said Shapiro. "Who do you think did it?"

"Who do I think killed Laura? Well, the roof of that motel office runs up to just beneath the window of the room where Mick and Laura were staying. The window was open. For the moment the police are going on the assumption that someone made it onto the roof of that office, which would have been easy, and slipped into the room and killed Laura while Mick was out at the front door with us. It could have happened that way. That means it *could* have been a prowler, but that's really stretching coincidence. I like to do things the hard way. It could have been Jeremy and/or Keith Terrance. Keith is supposed to be very handy with a knife. Or maybe Mick killed her before he answered the door. It could have happened that way too."

Shapiro pulled the rental car into a parking slot and braked to a halt. He killed the engine and grabbed his keys from the ignition. When he twisted to face Madison there was a cold fury in his expression and voice.

"When I came up with that crazy idea about there maybe being a psycho on these tours, I might just as well have gone up and scream-fed it into every T.V. camera in the country," he snarled. "I could have at least saved myself a little bread that way. What the hell have you been doing to earn the money I pay you, Madison?"

Madison's voice was frosty, too. "You can hold off on the employer crap, Arn. You've got a full refund coming, okay? I screwed up this one real good, and it cost someone their life. A very nice someone. I wouldn't take any money for what's going to happen next, anyway."

Some of Shapiro's bluster seemed to disappear. "And what's going to happen next?" he asked almost cautiously.

"Whoever killed Laura is going to answer to *me*," said Madison.

The last word was a snarl. Connie Frazer leaned

forward and touched his shoulder. "Steve, you can't blame yourself—"

"I can, and I do," he told them both. "I was trying to play God and shift people's lives around. I've done it before and pulled it off okay. But this time one of the lives got lost. I'm going to find the bastard that killed her. Then I'm going to play God one more time. All for free. Then maybe I'll be able to look at myself in the mirror again."

He opened his door and climbed from the car.

Arn Shapiro appeared taken aback by the quiet emotion of Madison's words. He looked like a man who wanted to say something but wasn't sure just what.

Connie started to follow Madison out of the car. He stopped her with a hard glance.

"Steve, I'm a part of this. I have a right to come with you."

"I thought you didn't believe in an eye for an eye." Shapiro finally found his voice.

"Steve, maybe I did come on a little strong. It's not just the money, you should know that. I only met Laura a few times when the band was up to the office in New York, but she seemed like a fine person. Hell, I don't want to see anyone killed. If you go off half-cocked—"

Madison closed the car door after him. He leaned forward to look at Shapiro through the open window.

"The time for playing both ends against the middle is way past, Arn. You must have figured out the score as well as I have. There's no way it can be done quietly. I'm sorry but that's the way it is."

Connie was still leaning forward from the back. "I've earned my right to share this assignment," she said.

"You have," nodded Madison. "I owe you a lot, lady. But I don't owe getting you killed."

"I can handle myself. I've proven that. Don't I have the right to choose?"

"Not this time, and I'm sorry about that, too. I care too much about you, Connie. I'd be worrying about you even if I didn't need to. I'd be careless—or *too* careful—and that could get us both killed. You've got to let me handle this on my own. I hope you understand that."

She relaxed back into the car. Her eyes told him that she didn't want it this way—but that she cared enough about him in return to respect even a wish like this one..

Not so Shapiro. "At least let me tag along, wherever the hell you're going," gruffed the promoter. "Don't forget who's paying the bills."

"No one's paying the bills," said Madison. "This one's on me, remember?"

He turned and started toward the motel. He could feel their eyes following his back all the way. A part of him wanted to turn around, go back to them, but he didn't.

This was nothing he could turn from. Threatening banks of dark rain clouds were gathering to the west, moving in over the city. A storm was brewing. Even the sunshine seemed chilly.

Madison entered the Holiday Inn, feeling the chill to his very soul—and knowing that it had nothing to do with the weather.

1 3

IT HAPPENED IN THE ELEVATOR.

It all began to catch up with him.

The impatience to be *doing* something after all those hours of police questioning was a very real thing, sure. But the energy of that impatience alone could only propel him so far. Then he would need to rely on defensive senses that would have to be awake and honed, and on-reflexes which would need to be clean and automatic. But he had been pushing nonstop since eight o'clock the previous evening. Not so long in hours, maybe, but an eternity to his now exhausted body and mind.

But he could not slow down. He would not allow himself to. In Nam he'd learned the hard way that when it was a matter of immediate personal danger, the inner survival instincts rarely failed to perform, no matter how tired the conscious mind might think itself.

He would have to trust his own capabilities. There were no other options open to him. No, he would not slow down. Not *now*. No way.

The members of The Screaming Tree were registered anonymously on the twelfth floor of The Holiday Inn. The anonymity was to insure their privacy from persistent fans. It was now probably hoped by Lee Brocchi that the anonymity would also accomplish the secondary purpose of somewhat covering their tracks from the media after all the excitement of that morning.

If, that is, the band was even returning to the motel.

Madison was alone in the elevator. As the car came to a stop and the doors yawned open, his faith in himself was rewarded as his fatigue seemed to evaporate and all his senses went on *Alert*.

He left the elevator, walking down the carpeted hallway toward the room shared by Keith Terrance and Mick Adamson. He moved briskly yet with a loose-jointed caution, his right hand held close to the body, ready to dart beneath the jacket toward the .44 Magnum at a moment's notice.

He didn't know what to expect, not even of himself. What was coming, if the band had indeed returned to their rooms, would resemble a musical jam in that it would be played strictly by ear, carefully watching and listening to each of the others before deciding what lines you yourself would use.

There were some things about this assignment that Madison knew, others he could only guess at and still many more that he would like to know. Now was the time to ask, before emotions and fears and paranoia could cool and new lies could be thought up.

He reached the door and knocked sharply. Two seconds passed. The door was yanked open by Brocchi. "Goddammit, no interv—" His intense dark eyes went from flashing to narrow. "Madison!"

Madison slipped into the room. It was one of those big open ones with two double beds. Madison took a quick inventory of the faces present.

"Well, well," he said. "The gang's all here."

Jeremy Bates was closest to him. The new widower was leaning against the shelf beneath the wall mirror. He was holding a fifth of Jack Daniels and he looked morose and restless in equal proportions. Across the room, Mick Adamson sat hunched forward in a low chair beside the window. His elbows were on his knees and he was staring at the carpet like a man who wished he was invisible. Between the widower and the wiry lead singer, Keith Terrance sat on the end of one of the double beds with his feet planted squarely on the floor and his muscles bulging under a tight T-shirt. Madison had the impression that the big drummer's positioning was more strategic than by chance.

Terrance turned slightly, glaring at the new arrival.

"Get the hell out of here, Madison. This is a private wake. No promo men needed."

Madison nodded from Jeremy to Mick.

"These two don't exactly seem to be enjoying each other's company," he said. "What's keeping them here if it isn't your muscle? I don't think you'd take the trouble for a wake, Keith. You might for a business conference, though."

Brocchi stepped forward.

"There is some business to take care of," he said. His manner implied that this was his turf and that he had the situation well under control, but that he was willing to take Madison into his confidence. "It's something only the guys can decide. Whether or not to play their scheduled show tonight."

Madison felt a jab of anger in the pit of his stomach that began to extend all over his chest.

"Say that again," he said slowly.

Over in the chair, Mick Adamson came to life, addressing everyone but Madison. "I say we have no business playing tonight," he snarled. "This is carrying the-show-must-go-on bullshit a little too far if you ask me."

"So, rib one's asking you," Keith Terrance told him coolly. "We're professional musicians and we've got a job to do. You're just feeling like a piece of shit and you don't want the world looking at you. But if it isn't too heavy for Jeremy to play tonight, I don't see where you even have a say in the matter." Madison shifted his attention to Jeremy Bates. The lead guitarist lifted his arm and downed a long hit from the bottle. He glared back at Madison almost defiantly.

"Laura knew me," he said. "She knew what was important to me. She always told me to do what was right. Those people who have tickets to our show tonight...they want us to share our music with them. That's important. Laura was a musician's woman and she'd understand that."

Madison paused for a moment. Every word that Jeremy had said was true. Yet something within him was still offended by what was going down here.

"It seems like respect for the dead should come into it somewhere along the line," he said evenly.

Mick Adamson burst from his chair and stepped forward but remained on the other side of Terrance. He pointed an accusing finger at Madison.

"See! That's what I've been talking about! Look at the way he keeps playing us against each other!"

"Yeah," agreed Terrance, eyeing Madison. "When we had our talk on the plane yesterday—"

"Is that what you're calling it now, Keith—a talk?" The drummer continued as if he hadn't been interrupted. "We never did get it straight just who you are, Madison. Maybe now would be a real good time to tell us."

Madison nodded.

"Maybe it would." He looked at Brocchi. "Tell them, Lee."

Brocchi's expression seemed to tighten, but Terrance didn't notice it..

"Why don't you just stop messing with people's heads?" the drummer shouted angrily. "You tried to turn me and Lee against each other back at the airstrip. It didn't take then, and it won't take now. He's Jeremy's main man and that's good enough for me.".

"It was good enough for Shapiro too," said Madison. "Lee and I have been working side by side since Chicago."

Brocchi stepped forward. The simmering rage that Madison had recognized as far back as the police department was now brimming over.

"Madison, you two-faced sonovabitch—"

Madison stood his ground. His fingertips hovered near the front of his jacket, very close to the butt of the .44.

Brocchi got the hint and stopped.

Madison looked around at all four of them.

"So, you're having a wake for Laura," he said. "While you're at it, how about a wake for the girl who died in Chicago two nights ago? Or all the other girls on all the other Screaming Tree tours?"

Across the room, Mick Adamson looked mildly stunned.

"What the hell's he talking about?" he demanded of the others.

Jeremy took another sip of Jack Daniels.

"I'd say the dude's just playing us off against each other, Mick. Watch yourself." Madison looked at Brocchi.

"Watch yourself?" he mimicked, turning it into a question. "How much have you told these boys already, Lee?"

"There was a murder last night," the road manager bristled. "You want it straight? Okay. That man's wife was killed and every man in this room is wondering who killed her. There's a lot that no one's had the guts to talk about or suggest yet. Yeah, everyone's being real careful about what they say!" From the bed, Keith Terrance was glaring at Brocchi.

"Let Jeremy take care of himself," he said. "Why don't you tell us what Madison's talking about, Lee? You told me yesterday on the plane that you didn't know anything about that girl's murder in Chicago that Madison was telling me about. What have you got to say now? What's this about you and Madison working together?"

"All right, everyone's letting their hair down all of a sudden," said Brocchi. "I'll do the same." He looked at Madison. "But I want this sonovabitch out before I do."

"That's good enough for me," agreed Mick from across the room. "We used to all be pretty tight with each other before this bastard Madison joined the tour."

Keith Terrance stood and faced Madison. The drummer's hefty form seemed to fill the space between the two beds.

"I think it's about time we got back to the business at hand," he said.

His tone implied that this statement should be sufficient as both a suggestion and a threat.

Jeremy Bates pushed himself upright from where he'd been leaning. He was still holding the whiskey bottle—only now it looked like it could become a weapon.

"I can tell that you've been touched by my wife's

death," he told Madison solemnly. "I appreciate you stopping by. But we do have things to talk over. Personal things. So why don't you split? You grieve your way—we'll grieve in ours, okay?"

Lee Brocchi cast the final vote and he did it without a word. He crossed over to the door and held it open for Madison.

Madison did another inventory of the faces of the three band members, as he had when he stepped in. There was no way of ignoring the determination set into each one's expression. There were four of them—and Brocchi had a gun.

"Someone in this room is a murderer," Madison said quietly. "But he's not going to murder anyone else. Does everyone here understand that?"

"Forget the exit speeches," sneered Terrance. "You sound like a Charlie Chan movie. Lee's got the door—be on your way."

As Madison, passed Brocchi, he said to the road manager in a low voice, "Relax, I got you back in solid with the boys, didn't I?"

There was a glint of satisfaction along with the hate in Brocchi's intense eyes.

"You conned me, Madison," he admitted. "Jeremy was my friend and I almost turned rat on him. But Mick is right. You've just been playing head games with everybody." He nodded toward the band members. "I'm going to level with these guys," he said. "Just like I should have in the first place. *Then* we'll try and put together what happened last night—and we'll do it between the four of us. Now split."

Madison stepped into the hallway and was glad to hear the door slam shut behind him. Once by himself, he began smiling as he walked on down the corridor.

Yeah, he was playing head games, and he wasn't anywhere near done, either. The pot that he'd been stirring since his arrival on the tour in Chicago was now ready to boil over, just like it was supposed to. Madison had pushed these men, had pressed all their paranoia buttons, had coldly played them against each other without any show of favoritism, solely to get them to this. He had them all up against the wall now. Whoever the killer was among the four of them was watching his whole little card house come tumbling down, because the pressure wouldn't be off the others until the murderer was caught.

They were pulling in their ranks. But that wouldn't help. It was too late for that now. Madison had them all in objective focus. Waiting. When the psycho among them finally panicked and bolted and revealed himself, Madison would be ready, and the game would be over.

One way or another.

Rounding a hallway corner, he decided to pay a call on Connie Frazer in her room, two down from his own.

He remembered yesterday afternoon when he had been on his walk back to the Holiday Inn from his talk with Mick. That seemed like eons ago now. But he did remember two things quite distinctly: seeing Connie Frazer drive off with Jeremy Bates—and experiencing an admittedly unjustifiable pang of jealousy at the sight. Maybe the second part was meaningless soap opera stuff after everything else that had happened. Madison was prepared to admit that this might be the case. But he did want to find out what had been discussed on that drive.

As his defenses relaxed somewhat from the meeting with the band, some of his fatigue returned. But he tried to blank it from his mind, refusing to slow down. He still had to be doing something. He owed that much to the memory of what he and Laura had once had.

She'd been right, that last time they'd spoken, yesterday afternoon in the motel cocktail lounge. She still held a special place in his heart that would always be hers alone. The memory of the love they had shared was a sacred thing. Her death would be avenged.

But at the same time, Madison knew enough to distinguish duty to the dead from his own flowing life forces.

He wanted to see how Connie's head was doing. He wanted to see how she was, without Arn Shapiro lending an ear to every word.

He knocked on her door a few times but there was no answer.

It hadn't been more than ten minutes since he'd left Connie and Shapiro down in the parking lot. It didn't make sense that they'd immediately split up. Her original assignment had been to keep an eye on Madison for Shapiro, whether she knew it or not. Madison wasn't willing to guess whether Shapiro would decide she'd been a howling success or a miserable failure. But he did realize that Shapiro would want Connie to render a full report immediately. Madison could probably take the elevator down and catch them right now in the bar.

He had to pass his own room on his way to the elevator. He did a quick mental placement of everybody. Brocchi and the members of The Screaming Tree were back in Mick and Keith's room, keeping an eye on each other. Shapiro and Connie Frazer were either downstairs or off in some other bar or restaurant, discussing the case. He'd known Shapiro long enough to know that the promoter might indeed be a bloodsucker in some ways, but he was no raving psycho..

Madison also knew that there was only one thing he needed now to refresh himself; to purge the fatigue and deliver fresh energy so he could keep on doing things. No one in the scenario would miss him snatching a ten-minute shower and a change of clothes.

He paused before his door, fitting his key into the lock.

His mind was busy turning over the various aspects of the case. Arn Shapiro's fear had been right from the very start. Someone in The Screaming Tree had a taste for blood. Brocchi could not be considered as guilty of the murder of Laura Bates. Laura's throat had just been slashed, her blood had been warm and pumping, when Madison discovered her corpse. Lee Brocchi had been by Madison's side since Madison had rousted him across town at the Holiday Inn. So, who did that leave? That's right, it was back to Square number one: which member of The Screaming Tree was it? Wiry, always high Mick Adamson? Big Keith, the Satanist freak? Or Jeremy, first the cuckold, then the widower?

Madison turned the doorknob and began to step into his room.

He sensed the shadowy movement from behind—
too late!

His last rational thought was that he should have listened to his body! That he had pushed himself too far after all. The physical fatigue was about to kill him.

Then the blow struck. It was hard, smashing, vicious. It caught him at the base of his neck. The universe exploded with a blinding flash and he pitched forward, into the room. He wasn't unconscious, but his senses were reeling. He hit the floor and rolled onto his back.

A figure moved into the apartment after him, closing the door behind him. Madison shook his head, trying to clear it, trying to make out the features of the man who was now approaching him., Madison was pushing himself to his feet when the next blow struck. The effect of the first hadn't worn off yet. The bastard's shoe nailed him beneath the jaw and pitched him onto his back again, waves of blinding pain washing over him. A pause—and a powerful kick to the side that seemed to tear his body in half.

He tried to push himself up with his elbows,

fighting the unconsciousness; the dark pit that was trying to pull him into it. He reached for the Magnum. The reflexes were numb with blinding pain, but still functioning.

But it all must have been happening faster than his mind could grasp. Reality was a warped, twisted thing.

His attacker, he now realized, had already stepped across the room to the single bed, and back. He was holding something, something big and bulky. He was standing over Madison, looking down, his features still foggy and shimmering and unclear.

Madison's fingertips moved beneath his jacket, covering those last inches toward the .44.

The guy was holding a pillow. It was supposed to muffle the shot!

It did.

Madison perceived the flash and the dull blast, the pillow jumping in the figure's grip and an exploding cloud of white as the feathers flew.

The sledgehammer strike against his chest was the final kick into utter, black oblivion.

Madison had one last horrible impression of what it was like to die.

1 4

ETERNITY WAS A SHRILL, RINGING SOUND. IT HAD BEEN pulling him from the grip of unconsciousness for as long as he could remember. Then, slowly, the other senses returned.

The pain was worse than anything he had ever known. His first instinctual response was to yearn for the tranquility of unconsciousness once again. But that was no good. He was coming awake in quickening degrees. The shrill sound that had brought him back was reduced to its rightful size in the universe.

The telephone was ringing.

Madison opened his eyes. The pain that had been stabbing at the side of his chest now spread, exploding within his skull. He realized that he was in his Holiday Inn room stretched out on the floor. Somehow coming back from the dead. And the phone was ringing.

The room tilted as he stood. He forced himself

forward, toward the pealing instrument. He snatched it up on what must have been its millionth ring.

"Steve?" a feminine voice asked tentatively.

"Yeah, Connie. It's me. What's left of me. Where are you calling from?"

The roar of a heavy truck engine from the background noise over the connection spoiled her reply. Madison pictured an outdoor pay phone near a highway.

"—for lunch," she was saying when the highway sounds behind her died down a moment later. "It's happening just like you thought it would. I'm going to tag

along and see what I can get."

Madison's mind was suddenly wide awake. "Connie, listen. Things have changed." He accented each word, giving each a special importance. "We're not playing *I Spy* with these guys anymore. The lid's blowing off. Someone just tried to kill me."

A gasp came over the wire.

"My god... then it's even more important that I stay with what I've got here. I'm okay. I've got my gun."

"Connie, where are you? Who is it?"

Another roaring engine from the highway behind her drowned out the reply. When the rumbling had died away, there was only silence over the wire.

Madison felt his stomach freeze into a tight knot.

"Hello...hello, Connie?'

The connection clicked in his ear. Then, only the monotonous hum of the dial tone.

He smashed the receiver back onto the phone and the movement sent lances of pain riding hotly, torturously across the entire left side of his body. The pain centered around his chest, just below and in front of his left arm.

Remembering now that he thought he'd been dying, he reached under his jacket for the wound.

There was no wound.

He pulled out the .44 Magnum. The weapon was as heavy and impressive as ever in his hand, but there was one difference. The thick, ornate butt was now a mangled mess. It had stopped a bullet. The Magnum had saved his life—but had been rendered useless in the process.

He pitched the wreckage onto the bed, then crossed to where his suitcase lay open on a low folding rack. Each step sent more jabs of pain hammering at the left side of his body. He could imagine what the flesh beneath his shoulder holster must look like: bruised, pulpy, and bones possibly broken. But imagining was enough. He wasn't about to slow down for a look.

He found the finished maple wood box containing the ruined .44's healthy twin under a pair of slacks, right where it was supposed to be. Checking the action and load, he holstered the new weapon. The slight pressure of the holster against the bruise sent more spasms of pain hammering through him. He stood for a moment, bracing himself. He would have to ignore the pain. He would function as if it didn't exist.

He left his room, moving down the motel hallway at a steady jog.

He glanced at his watch. It was three-thirty-four. No wonder he felt like he was coming back from the dead. No wonder he had fooled his "killer." He'd been out for most of the afternoon.

Yeah, *Saturday* afternoon...

His mind was working with a new idea, shaping the hunch in his gut into a concept which could be examined.

The killer had felt the pressure and snapped, all right. But just a tad ahead of schedule. Now he was bolting, and taking along as many with him as he could.

He had Connie. That could be the only explanation for that disconnected phone call. *So now the sick bastard has her.* He thinks he's killed Madison and now he has the lady—and he'll probably take his own sweet, sick time about the way in which; *she* dies.

Where would he take her? Madison thought he knew the answer. But first, there might be a more direct way of finding out.

He reached Lee Brocchi's door and slammed on it with his right fist. No response. He hurried down to the room shared by Mick and Keith. Again, no reply. He got the same at Jeremy Bates' door. He was just turning as Arn Shapiro rounded the corner. Shapiro glared, came forward.

"I don't believe it!" he growled peevishly. "I'm actually seeing a familiar face. Where the hell *is* everybody?'"

Madison ignored the question.

"When was the last time you saw Connie?" he asked quickly.

"After we dropped you off, we had lunch," said Shapiro. "We split up downstairs. She said that she was really wiped out from last night and needed to fall out for a while."

"That's the last time you saw her?"

"Yeah. She took the elevator up. I tried to find you later, but there was no answer at your door. And now the goddamn band and Brocchi have all disappeared on me. What the hell's going on around here, Madison?"

"I need your car keys," Madison told him. "I never recovered my wheels from last night—and I've got some important business to take care of."

Shapiro narrowed his still angry eyes, as if taking a quick, careful reading of the man before him. He grunted, then nodded at what he saw. He reached into his pocket and produced his car keys. But he held onto them.

"We're going together," he said. "The wire services have picked up what happened last night to Laura and all hell's breaking loose back in the New York office. I'm out here to be doing something, goddammit!"

Madison made a grab and snatched the keys.

"I told you before. I can't have anyone slowing me down, Arn."

Madison started to turn. The promoter wasn't

about to stand for that. He made a reach. "Give me those keys!" he snarled.

Madison turned back to face him.

"Sorry, Arn," he said sincerely.

He made a loose fist and swung. The knuckles connected with Shapiro's jaw loud enough to be heard down the hall. Shapiro's legs folded, and he went down.

Madison didn't bother with a backward glance. He didn't bother with waiting for the elevator, either. He took the stairs, sailing. He burst from the ground floor stairwell door to the outside and made a bee-line toward Shapiro's parked rental car.

The day had changed during the time he'd been unconscious. The rain clouds he'd noticed before off to the west were locked in over Kansas City now like a low, ominous roof. A chilled breeze carried the heavy scent of approaching rain.

He spun the car out of the parking lot and took off with a squeal, the rubber leaving long smoking patches behind him.

The hunch had crystallized. He was willing to bet that he knew exactly where this vampire psycho—whoever he was—had taken Connie Frazer. Hell, he *was* betting on it. He was betting the lady's life. The life he had promised to save if it ever needed saving.

It needed saving now, damned fast.

Madison wheeled from the parking lot into the flow of traffic, peeling more rubber from the squealing tires. He headed due north with the pedal down. If that fine woman died because he was wrong or too slow, he would pray to be damned to an Eternal Hell.

Overhead, mighty thunder rumbled from the low clouds, sounding like some hungry animal about to feast. As he steered through the traffic with his left hand, Madison drew the .44 with his right and placed it on the seat beside him, where it would be easier to reach._

The dark clouds rumbled again. Droplets of rain began beading on the windshield. Madison felt a sudden cosmic oneness with the universe around him. As if he were part of the approaching, stormy violence which was about to purge the city, flushing the filth and decay down into the gutter where it belonged.

THE FRONT GATES OF THE SLOAN GRAVEL COMPANY, flattened the night before by the homicidal dump truck, had been set upright again and loosely linked together. But it was a halfhearted job. Madison slid easily between them, thankful for not having to scale the top of the fence to gain entrance as he had on his previous visit. He was doing his best to live with the hammering discomfort of his almost- bullet-wound, but there seemed no sense in provoking it.

Once inside, he took off at a fast clip up the truck path which led on between the high gravel pyramids. The mini-mountains were shiny with moisture, cold-looking, foreboding. All about him, the grounds were still.

The big .44 Magnum was in his right fist, held tight and ready. His eyes were wary, scanning the dim valleys between the gravel pyramids as he continued along the dirt road.

The bottom hadn't dropped out from those hovering black rain clouds overhead yet, but it was still misting. The moisture was icy and unfriendly. Thunder was a constant, low rumbling sound from above. Jagged silver streaks of lightning slashed across the low, dark sky.

The sounds of traffic on Route One-Sixty-Nine drifted to him from beyond the fence, car tires singing on the wet pavement and the occasional roar of a passing heavy-duty truck rising above everything else.

A momentary sense of *deja vu* gripped him. Without slowing his pace he glanced back over a shoulder to make sure that no more behemoth dump trucks were piling down on him. He continued, deeper into the grounds. It was misting harder now. Harder and colder. Off to his left he saw the closest rim of what seemed to be an immense quarry.

The road curved to his right and he stayed on it.

He wasn't sure what he was looking for. But he would know when he saw it. If his hunch had been right.

The highway sounds from One-Sixty-Nine grew fainter, until the twisting valley between the gravel heaps became a world of its own. It was those now fading highway sounds that had brought him back here. He remembered Connie telling him that this was the first time that anyone on the tour had ever been to Kansas City. That meant that the killer had probably just picked the gravel quarry at random yesterday on the limo ride in from the airport. He wanted to waste Madison, to get him off his tail. Passing by, the quarry must have seemed like a good place. There hadn't been any time for much more scouting around. So when Madison had showed up here after dark last night, the killer had already taken the time to pick the lock on the front gates, had hotwired and stolen one of the dump trucks left on the grounds overnight, and had been waiting for Madison in the darkness near the highway, to watch him go in and smash him like a bug once he was inside. Now that the killer had more work to do— work that he would want to take his time with—why shouldn't he bring Connie back here?

The highway sounds that had kept drowning out crucial parts of Madison's last phone conversation with Connie also played a part in his being here. He remembered that certain stretches of Highway One- Sixty- Nine were lined with all manner of restaurants. How much like this sick killer it would be, after he thought he'd killed Madison, to slip on his mask of normalcy one more time, just to get his hands-on Connie? Any man looking at her would wish that he could possess her once before he died. She was that kind of magical woman. And a madman could make it happen.

A madman *was* making it happen! He had even taken her to lunch, letting the condemned eat a hearty meal. The guy would really get off, watching her enjoy her meal with no idea that it was to be her last.

And he would bring her here. Construction always shuts down on weekends. So do gravel quarries. The

Sloan Gravel Company was perfect for what the guy would have on his mind.

The winding dirt road curved once again between two pyramids of gravel. Then a clearing came into view. In the middle of the clearing, trucks and machinery were parked around a cheaply constructed one room office/shack.

Madison saw a dim light from the side window, shimmering through the mist.

The mist had become a drizzle, the cold breeze whistling through the canyons between the gravel heaps. Madison was soaked to the skin. He moved forward to keep warm, running, keeping low.

This was it.

The single window was next to the door. He glided in against the shack, between window and door. He crouched, pressing flat against the building.

He raised his right arm, thumbing the Magnum onto full cock. Then he lifted an ear toward the window. It was open an inch at the bottom. He listened for voices.

At first, the rumbling of thunder from overhead blotted out everything else.

Then he heard the whimpering.

They were the sounds of a woman in torment, weak with pain, pleading and total humiliation.

"No... please...not *that!*"

And another voice. A voice more growling beast than human, intoning an obscene litany in-low, passion-choked tones.

"For the Lord God Satanus, I give to you the hot living blood of this woman, your daughter—"

Madison stood up and faced the shack door. He aimed a powerful kick at the cheap panel of wood and sent it sailing from its hinges. He stepped inside—and winced at the sight before him,

Connie Frazer was nude, strung up to the ceiling by a long, rubberized length of line, drawn taut onto her tiptoes. She swayed slowly around in an unnatural, slow motion pirouette. Madison's senses flared with rage at what he saw.

He had feasted on her. No more than small bite marks, but hundreds of them. Most of her body was covered with droplets of blood; those he had missed with his tongue...

She swayed around and saw Madison, and her uncontrollable gasp was what alerted the naked man who had been turning and fondling her.

Lee Brocchi spun around in a low animal crouch. The road manager's muscular body was matted with coal-black hair. Blood was smeared across his mouth and hands.

Outside, the storm unleashed itself. The walls of the shack shuddered to the mightiest roar of thunder yet. Lightning blazed. The silvery flash from the doorway behind Madison was a reflected glint in the madman's eyes.

Brocchi charged from across the room, still crouching, fingers clenched.

Madison lifted the Magnum and sighted down his arm's length.

"This is for Laura," he said evenly. "And for all of the others, you bastard."

Brocchi's mouth ripped open in what should have been a snarl. But the snarl never came.

Madison squeezed off a round with deadly precision, stopping Brocchi in mid-stride. The slug took the guy at the bridge of the nose and blew his head apart. Grayish pink semi-liquids and chips of bone sprayed the air. Some of it splattered across Connie Frazer's body like splashed paint.

Connie looked down at the wet shiny mess across her bare thighs. Then she looked at the nearly headless body of Lee Brocchi that seemed to take two or three steps backward of its own volition before becoming a pile of dead matter in a corner across the room. Then her mouth twisted apart in a scream that must have been yanked from her very soul. Her head bobbed forward onto her chest, her blonde hair a golden cascade.

Mercifully, she had lost consciousness.

Madison bolstered the .44. He produced a penknife and approached the woman, cutting at her bonds. There was a couch against the far wall. Madison lifted Connie Frazer into his arms and carried her over to it, setting her down gently.

The only sound was the pouring rain rattling on the shack's tin roof. A welcomed breeze blew in from the shattered doorway, smelling clean and fresh.

Madison wasted a quick glance at what was left of Lee Brocchi, The Screaming Tree's road manager,

Madison felt fulfilled. This was the guy the vampire chase had been all about. It had been a pleasure to send him to Hell to his beloved Lucifer. They deserved each other.

Connie's clothes were scattered around the floor of the shack. Madison began gathering them up. He would have to help her dress and see to it that her injuries were attended to. Then he had one more stop to make.

The vampire chase was almost over.

Almost...

The storm had passed by the time Madison pulled into the crowded parking lot of Mun Stadium, just off Interstate Seventy east of Kansas City. The ground was damp, but the air was fresh and clean. It was nine-o-five.

The sounds of a rock band in full flight drifted out to him front within the stadium. That would be the last warmup band to go on before the star attraction, and they were probably good for another twenty-five minutes. That would give the roadies thirty minutes to shuffle around the equipment. The Screaming Tree had been scheduled to appear at ten.

Madison walked through the darkness, between the lines of cars, toward the front gate. His tour credentials got him through easily.

Before circling around to the backstage area, he paused for a moment at the top of one of the aisles to the rear of the audience. He stood scanning the packed stadium with tired eyes. It was a sight that never failed to impress: seventy thousand screaming, boogying fans, moving and grooving on the same wave length with driving musicians who were barely specks on the stage from this distance. But that didn't matter. It was the *spirit* of boogying together that was important. Madison's generation had learned that at Monterey and Woodstock. It was what rock 'n roll was all about. A loud, loose, sharing celebration of the joys of life. And this crowd was into that trip completely, having a ball with the soaring music and with each other. To them, Laura Bates was only a name in the newspapers. They were here to have fun.

Madison turned from the celebration of life and continued along the concourse toward the backstage section, his mind occupied with thoughts of death. He was walking slowly but purposefully. There was no hurry now.

The police had not liked his story, but they had seemed to believe it. At least as far as they were letting on. They were holding onto his gun, but after five hours of interrogation he had been released. He had kept the vampire angle out of it, as well as the tie-in with the murder of Laura Bates. As far as the police were concerned, Lee Brocchi had kidnapped Connie Frazer for obvious reasons and Madison had come to her rescue with equally obvious results. The physical evidence had been enough to sell them on the story, but Connie backing Madison up every step of the way had helped too. As had the general feeling among the investigating staff that rock stars and their assorted flacks were no damn good. What did they expect, doing all those drugs all the time? The consensus seemed to be that Brocchi's death was sordid but understandable, par for the game he'd played and the company he'd kept.

Connie Frazer would be all right. She was resting in the hospital at this very minute, listed in Satisfactory Condition. The bite wounds inflicted by Lee Brocchi were numerous but mostly superficial and were not expected to leave scars.

The scars would all be inside.

Madison used his I.D. to get backstage. The dressing room area was every bit as crowded as the one back in Chicago at Soldier Field had been, when Madison had heard The Screaming Tree for the first time. But there was a difference. There was no partying going on here. Backstage among the musicians and their followers, the death of a fellow musician's wife was a real thing. People weren't exactly standing around weeping—few of them probably knew her and, after all, the gig must go on—but even arriving late as he was, the muted energies and general lack of horse-play were noticeable to Madison, contrasting sharply the festive atmosphere out front.

He elbowed his way through the tightly grouped clusters of people, not even slowing down. The Screaming Tree's dressing room door came into view. Two burly rent-a-cops guarded the door, one on either side. But it was late in a long evening and they both looked tired.

Madison stepped between them before either one could fully react. They were just turning as he slammed the door in their faces. He paused to throw the lock, then turned to face the dressing room.

Four men stared back at him. The three members of America's leading occult rock band and their manager, Arn Shapiro.

Jeremy Bates, Keith Terrance and Mick Adamson were done out in their full rock regalia: the black leather jump suits, the high-heeled platform boots, the slashes of iridescent "lighting" arching across their costumes, and their faces dyed wild colors, beneath frizzed-out hair.

They were huddled around in a small circle, as if in the middle of an important meeting. Madison noticed none of the electricity usually crackling in a dressing just prior to showtime.

The band remained seated, glaring, at the interruption, Shapiro rose and faced Madison.

"You've got your nerve showing up here," he rasped. He touched his jaw. "What was the idea of slugging me back there at the motel?"

"I told you I had to work solo," said Madison. "You just didn't want to listen to sense, remember?"

"I remember all too clearly. I don't like being kept out of things, dammit. Did you know about Brocchi when you left me lying unconscious there on the floor? Where the hell have you been since three-thirty?'

"In a minute," said Madison. He nodded toward the

band. "There sure are a lot of meetings going on today. What's this one about?"

"We've been patching things up," said Shapiro. "Brocchi is the one who's been killing all of these women. The guy's a homicidal nut. He pulled a gun on these guys this afternoon and threatened to kill them."

Madison looked at the band members. "Is that why you disappeared from the motel?"

Keith fielded the question. "Things were coming totally apart," said the hefty drummer. "We had to get away by ourselves and sort things out between the three of us."

"You could have tried calling the cops."

"We didn't know about you and your vampire at the time," said Mick Adamson irritably. "After you split from our room this afternoon, we expected Brocchi to sit down and talk." The lead singer was up and moving around as he spoke, wired as usual. "But the first thing he does after closing the door is to pull a gun and tell everyone he'll waste the first dude who tries to follow him."

"And there weren't any heroes, huh?"

"He had a gun, Madison," said Jeremy Bates wearily.

Madison touched his own side, wincing at the pain. "Yeah, I guess he did," he agreed. "So, you spent some time laying low and getting your heads together and now you're here to play the gig, is that it? Just like nothing's happened?"

"I explained that to you this afternoon," said Jeremy flatly. It was as if the events of that day and the preceding night had used up all his emotion. "Laura was a musician's woman. It's the way she would have wanted it. She'd understand."

Madison turned to Shapiro.

"The police just released me," he reported. "I killed Brocchi this afternoon."

The promoter flinched as if he'd been struck. His ulcer must have been giving him hell. "Run that by me again, slowly," he said.

"He went off the deep end," said Madison: "After he left these guys he ran down to my room and tried to kill me. He must have figured I was the root of all his trouble. He thought he had killed me, for a while there. Then he went after Connie. He couldn't have gone on much longer. He must have been hip to that all along. When his time came, he wanted to go out in style."

Mick Adamson stopped moving around and sank back into his chair. The singer and bassist was still keeping his distance from Jeremy, keeping Keith Terrance between them. "How much do the police know?' he asked. "I've had my fill of cops."

"I squared it with the police," Madison told them. "The vampire angle doesn't come into it at all. As far as the K.C.P.D. is concerned, what happened this afternoon was a one-time thing. A crime of passion. They already think Brocchi went crazy on drugs and maybe he did. But the case is closed."

Terrance was shaking his head. "I can remember Lee asking about the occult," he said, his voice dull with shock. "We used to rap about it a lot but... wow, it's really hard to believe."

"I thought I knew the guy," agreed Jeremy. "We were supposed to be buddies. Then something like this happens."

"I'm just glad it's over," said Mick. "Man, will I be glad to get onstage again and let loose."

"There won't be any letting loose tonight," said Madison. "Or any other night. Not with this band."

"What are you talking about?" demanded Shapiro. "That was a terrible tragedy, what happened to Laura. But if Jeremy wants to go on—"

Madison turned to Jeremy. "I wanted to get down here tonight before you went out and played," he said. "Laura might have wanted you to play tonight, I'll buy that—*except* for the way she died."

Keith Terrance sat erect. "Maybe you'd better explain what you're talking about, Madison," he suggested.

"He's still playing his damn head games," put in Adamson. Now that the heat was off he'd lost all interest in getting along with anybody. "Let's get those rent-a-cops in here and toss his ass out." Madison was still facing Jeremy.

"Laura died looking into her husband's eyes," he continued. "The show's over, Jeremy. You killed Laura and you're going to the slammer for it." Jeremy Bates rose to his feet. The elaborate stage makeup could not conceal the tightening muscles or the sudden keen interest of his expression.

"I don't quite follow you," he said softly.

"Then I'll spell it out. Brocchi was the vampire, but he didn't kill Laura. Laura's body was still warm when I found it. But Brocchi had been at my side for nearly a half hour before that. You killed her, Jeremy. You slipped into that motel room she was sharing with Mick and you slashed her throat while Mick was at the front door with us. Then you raced back to the Holiday Inn to hang out with Keith while you waited for the cops to bring you the bad news. You put on such a good "distraught husband" number they even let you go. But it was you, Jeremy, and you're going to pay."

Jeremy shook his head. "You're completely out of your mind," he said. "This is the craziest thing I've ever heard."

Arn Shapiro looked like a man who's used to making snap decisions, who suddenly finds himself not knowing what to do or what to think.

"Do you have anything to back this up, Steve?"

"Enough," said Madison. "In Chicago at the party that night after the gig, I made the mistake of telling Brocchi that he should check with you regarding why I joined the tour. Once he knew that much, though, he didn't have to check. He was shrewd enough to pick up that I was no promo man very early in the game, and he added that up only one way. Even if we didn't know who the vampire was, we were closing in. Lee decided to take immediate steps to protect himself by getting me out of the picture. Maybe then he thought the whole thing would slide by."

"That still doesn't say how Jeremy had anything to do with it."

"That night at the party," said Madison, "Keith left with that girl and I followed them. Brocchi followed me—and he brought Jeremy along. Jeremy had gone up to his room, but Brocchi could take the time to get him. Part of the band's contract was that Brocchi had to know where each one of them went at all times." Madison looked at Jeremy. "Lee made up the story that I was a narc and you bought it," he said. "You went along with him, out to the North Side where Keith had taken his groupie. At the time you probably thought you were helping Lee to save Keith from a drug bust." From behind his iridescent makeup, Keith Terrance's eyes were smoldering.

"She was a nice lady," he said to Jeremy. "You had no right to kill her, man."

"I didn't kill anybody, dammit," said Jeremy. "Not Laura and not anybody else. This guy's full of shit."

Madison ignored the interruption.

"When you got to that girl's house," he told Jeremy, "Brocchi had you sneak up behind me and lay me out cold. Then you stayed there to watch me while he went inside and hustled Keith back to the hotel. You were supposed to slug me again if I started waking up, right? What musician ever had any love in his heart for a narc? Brocchi probably told you that he had an idea that would expose me and embarrass me right off the tour and you were all for that. But when he came back he went inside the house and cold-bloodedly killed that girl right in front of your eyes, probably before you could stop him, and set it up as if I'd done it and it was a drug kill. I'm guessing that you were innocent up to that point or you'd have wasted me right at first when you came up behind me. But now—as Brocchi surely reminded you—you were his accomplice whether you liked it or not; an accessory to murder." From across the room, Mick Adamson was showing a renewed interest in the proceedings.

"But even if what you're saying is true," he interjected, "why should Lee go through all that trouble to tie Jeremy in with him?"

"He needed help in Chicago to get me out of the way," replied Madison. "The way it worked, he knew damn well that Jeremy wouldn't open his mouth and that's the kind of cooperation Brocchi wanted. He tried for me again last night at the gravel quarry and he used his hold over Jeremy one more time to get Jeremy to help him. And he repaid Jeremy by telling him that you were screwing his wife across town."

Madison turned and addressed Jeremy directly again. "Connie Frazer told me about your savage streak on our first night in Chicago," he said. "Brocchi must have known about it too. He also knew right where Mick and Laura were bedded down. I remember him giving me directions as we drove there last night. He gave directions to you, too, didn't he, Jeremy, after the two of you split from trying to waste me at the quarry? He knew exactly what you'd do when you heard about Mick and Laura. Maybe he just wanted to cement your partnership. Now he'd have a murder over your head that you'd actually committed. Or maybe he knew he was finished by that time and just wanted to take everyone else down with him. Whatever, you did just like you were supposed to. You stormed across town in a blind rage and murdered your wife for sleeping with another man."

"I still haven't heard anything I'd call proof," said Jeremy.

"The proof is on every tape recorder and video machine that was running this morning when you attacked Mick in the hallway of the police station," Madison told him. "Those hysterics of yours were all part of the grieving husband routine. You accused Mick of killing your wife and of trying to kill me, remember? The only hitch is that the police hadn't told anyone about the attack on me at the quarry at that point. So how did you know it...unless *you were a part of it?*"

Arn Shapiro stared at Jeremy in disbelief. "Jeremy, is this true?"

Jeremy responded promptly, but not with words.

Shapiro was standing between Jeremy and Madison. The lead guitarist grabbed Shapiro's arm and pitched him at Madison. The heavyset promoter was caught completely off guard. He piled into Madison, hard, and the two of them rocked back against Keith and Mick.

Jeremy darted from the room.

Madison untangled himself. He charged in pursuit.

"He's all mine." he called over his shoulder.

"Somebody phone the police!"

The hallway outside the dressing room was still choked with people. But between their heads Madison could make out Jeremy madly forcing his way toward the nearest exit. The two dumb rent-a-cops were standing next to Madison with their mouths open. Everyone else in the hallway was in the same state, looking around, trying to get out of the way, wondering what the hell was happening.

Madison shoved and pushed his way through the crowd. He suddenly realized that he was unarmed. The cops had taken his gun?

He swore fluently. But he didn't slow down. It didn't look like Jeremy was armed either.

Jeremy charged through a doorway; The pounding, driving rock music from onstage was immediately louder. The nearest doorway to the dressing room had been the one leading out to the stage— and that was the escape route Jeremy was taking.

Madison was right behind him. He burst through the doorway seconds later, onto the stage.

Onstage, the music was deafening. The band was still ripping through their hit songs. The band members had seen Jeremy—so had the audience— but it takes more than someone dashing across a stage to stop a rock concert. The roadies, who were supposed to keep things like this from happening, appeared to be in a state of shock. All they'd needed was one look at Jeremy's stage outfit to know who he was. Musicians are gods to the crews who handle the equipment, and they didn't know how to react.

Jeremy Bates showed no signs of slowing down. He was running across the full length of the stage as fast as his platform boots would carry him.

Madison raced after him, brushing by the performing band's lead guitarist. In addition to the axe the guy was strumming, the guitarist had three additional instruments lined up on stands behind him. Without slowing, Madison grabbed the nearest guitar by its neck.

Closing in on Jeremy, he twirled the guitar above his head like a war club and let fly.

Jeremy Bates glanced over his shoulder just as he reached the far end of the stage—and the sailing, rounded body of the heavy electric guitar caught him full-force in the forehead.

The band's music had finally begun tapering off as Jeremy spun and pitched from the high stage onto the sidelines.

He was still out cold when Madison reached him.

16

BRIGHT SHAFTS OF SUNLIGHT STABBED IN THROUGH THE hospital window, intensifying the stark whiteness of the room and all its furnishings.

Connie Frazer sat propped up in bed against the headboard. She seemed no worse for the wear of last night. The smile was strong and fresh. The skin tone and the eyes were bright with the spark of life.

Madison sat on the edge of the bed, and he had been doing most of the talking.

Arn Shapiro was due to catch a flight back to New York within an hour. But it was his suggestion that he accompany Madison on this visit, and that Madison relate to Connie the events of the previous night which she had missed. The promoter wasn't about to leave until he heard the last line, and Madison suspected that Shapiro just wanted to see if there was anything he'd missed the first few times he'd heard the story.

During the telling, Connie Frazer's hand had

slipped across the bedcovers and into Madison's. Her fingers seemed to make his palm tingle with their vibrant warmth.

He gave the hand a squeeze as he finished up with the events at Mun Stadium.

"And that's about it," he concluded. "The floor is open for questions."

"Just two," said Connie. "How did Brocchi and Jeremy find out about your meeting with Mick at the quarry the other night, so they could be there waiting for you?"

"I think I can answer that one," said Shapiro. "Mick told Laura, Laura must have told Jeremy. And Jeremy told Brocchi." He looked at Madison. "Right?'"

"Close enough. I'm sure Laura didn't make a point of mentioning it, but somehow it must have slipped out during a conversation between them and Jeremy was quick enough to pick up on it."

"Second question," said Connie. "When did you first suspect that Jeremy had killed Laura?"

"Not until after I'd learned that Brocchi was our vampire," said Madison. "Someone else had to have killed Laura and that's when I started thinking about Mr. Bates. Also, I couldn't ignore the vibes I picked up yesterday afternoon after we all got back from police headquarters, when the band and Brocchi were having their "wake-business conference" in Mick and Keith's room. After what had happened, Jeremy should have been trying to tear Mick's liver out. Think of it. Jeremy's wife had died that night in Mick's bed. But everything at the meeting was cool. Terrance probably thought that he was keeping Jeremy and Mick away from each other. Hell, Mick probably thought the same. But Jeremy was just doing his best to keep a low profile. He'd done his bit down at the police station to make himself look innocent when he attacked Mick there. Now he just wanted to flow with things and hope they'd blow over. Like I said, it just didn't play right. When I started thinking about it, everything else began falling into place.".

"You were a lot faster on the uptake than I was," said Connie. "I walked right into Brocchi's trap yesterday, didn't I? He came on so friendly. He started asking a lot of questions about you and what progress we were making for Arn on the assignment.

I remembered you saying in Chicago that he might try to play us off against each other and I decided to play him along and see what I could learn." She shook her head. "And boy! did I learn something!"

Madison gave her hand another squeeze. "That was last night," he said. "This is today, and the sun is shining. A good day for forgetting."

"Have you heard anything new about Jeremy?" Shapiro handled that one.

"He's copping a temporary insanity plea on Laura's murder," he said. "He's leaving out the vampire business. We all are."

"Jeremy would be a fool to bring that out," said Madison. "If he did, the murder of that girl in Chicago would probably be linked in and he'd have to explain his role in that. So, he's sitting tight, and that's fine with Arn. Right, Arn?"

"It could be worse," conceded Shapiro. "A kinky road manager and a love nest killing don't exactly make good press, but it sure beats hell out of a world-wide vampire spree. As long as Brocchi got his, and Jeremy's guaranteed on being locked away, what's the difference? Keith and Mick were the soul of The Screaming Tree anyway. They still are. The occult material is all theirs. That's what sold the group. They'll ride out the storm. Smaller groups have made it through worse ones. Then we'll get them another guitarist and we'll be back in business." He glanced at his watch. "Speaking of business, I've got a plane to catch. I've got The Eagles booked into the Garden tonight. Can't miss that one! Madison, you get crazier every time you work for me, but I can't bitch about the results. You earned your fifteen g's on this one. Connie, I'll see you in New York."

He gave a wave and started toward the door, audibly humming *Hotel California.*

"I've been trying to get out of this hospital all morning, Arn," Connie said after him. "They keep saying they're going to release me, but they don't say when. But I'll be back in the office by tomorrow morning, I promise."

Shapiro had already opened the door. He stood in the hallway, looking back into the room with one hand on the knob. He stopped humming for a moment.

"I said I'd see you in New York," he said. "I didn't say

when. You need relaxing and recuperating and plenty of it." He looked at Madison. "See that she gets it, Steve, if you want any more calls from me." Then he closed the door and was gone. He could be heard humming another Eagles song, growing fainter and fainter down the corridor.

Madison was still holding the lady's hand. Now that they were alone it felt even warmer, more vibrant, to his touch. "I've got a ranch outside of Durango," he told her. "Some Rocky Mountain air might be just what Dr. Shapiro ordered, Connie, if you'd care to join me for a week or two."

There was a pause that lasted longer than it should have. She seemed to be having trouble finding the right words. But find them, she did. "I'd just have to know one thing, Steve. You lost a woman on this tour who meant a lot to you. I think we could have a beautiful time in Durango. But I don't want to compete with a ghost. I don't want to think that the only reason I'm out here is to help you forget her."

"I lost Laura a long time ago," Madison told her. "It was a different person entirely that I met on this tour. I wasn't sure at first, but I am now. I felt bad for the person she'd become. I felt a lot of things and some of the feelings took me awhile to understand. But I didn't know her anymore. She told me that she'd become another person and she was right. We both had."

"I wish I could say the same for Jeremy," said Connie. "He asked me to go for a ride after we arrived in town yesterday. I told you that we'd been lovers, long ago. He still had that little boy smile that could melt your heart—and underneath he was still the same slimy creep. All he wanted was to use me the same way he used everyone else. He asked all kinds of questions about you and Brocchi. He seemed real concerned about what I knew about everybody on the tour. I guess he thought if the smile had conned me once, it would con me again."

"He was trying to keep his game straight after helping Brocchi in Chicago," said Madison. "I guess he figured you were his best bet."

"He asked me other things," said Connie. "He wanted to shack up. I—I almost puked. The whole lovey-dovey thing with Laura in front of others was just an act. I was so disgusted that I made him drop me off way on the other side of town. I couldn't even stand being in the same car with him. I had to walk by myself for half the afternoon before I felt clean again. He was still wearing that horrible boyish smile when he dropped me off. And before the night was over he was trying to kill you at that gravel quarry— and he *did* kill Laura!" She shuddered. "What a monster. I hope they never let him out."

"Lee Brocchi may have been a schizoid homicidal nut," said Madison. "But he did say one thing about Laura and what happened to her that made a lot of sense. She was the type of lady who gave everything she had to her man. When Jeremy started spitting on that, destroying it and throwing it back in her face, she just gave up and started sinking and soon she just didn't care anymore at all. That's when she tied up with Mick. Jeremy had killed her long before the other night, Connie."

"And now that he's been put away... can you say it's over, Steve? Can you turn your back on it and walk away?"

"I won't live in the past, lady," he assured her. "If you come to Durango with me I'll be there. Body, mind and spirit. That's a promise."

There was another pause. Then the lady's lush lower lip curved into a smile and seeming to make the bright hospital room even brighter.

"I just hope Arn knows what he's doing," she said with a musical laugh that matched the smile. "I've got a feeling that after Durango, I may never want to."

A LOOK AT FADE TO TOMORROW
(STEVE MADISON MYSTERIES)

BY STEPHEN MERTZ

In the title novel, As an Army Ranger, Steve Madison saw action from Iraq to Central America, from Somalia to Kosovo. But with his discharge from military service, he thought he'd seen the last of violence, bloodshed and sudden death. He was wrong.

As an "industrial consultant" to the music industry, Madison specializes in extricating pop stars from scandals that threaten to destroy multi-million-dollar careers. Johnny Willow is the hottest superstar of his generation; a young, gifted, blind musical genius whose addictions drove him into rehab and an extended hiatus at the height of his career. Now Johnny is back, clean and sober, with a new CD debuting at number one on the charts and a sold-out concert beginning a world tour. But one rainy night in St. Louis, Johnny's past returns with a vengeance and everything is threatened in a twisty maze of ghetto gang bangers, the Mafia, the DEA, a missing shipment of cocaine, kidnapping . . . and murder. That's where Steve Madison comes in.

In the short story, "A Hit for the New Age," when high-powered agent George Kodopolous is found murdered in a locked dressing room just before rock star Tony Jardeen's concert, Private Detective Steve Madison is hired to find out who did it—and comes face to face with a ghost from his past.

And, in "The Death Blues," a record producer comes to a private detective swearing he just heard a blues singer, who was supposed to be dead, alive and signing in a downtown club. But hen the detective is hired to find the man, he stumbles into a simmering neighborhood of anger and violence, and the only song he might be heading next is a funeral dirge.

AVAILABLE DECEMBER 2019 FROM Stephen Mertz AND WOLFPACK PUBLISHING.

ABOUT THE AUTHOR

Stephen Mertz is an American fiction author who is best known for his mainstream thrillers and novels of suspense. His work covers a wide variety of styles from paranormal dark suspense (*Night Wind* and *Devil Creek*) to historical speculative thrillers (*Blood Red Sun*) and hardboiled noir (*Fade to Tomorrow*). Mertz is also a popular lecturer on the craft of writing and has appeared as a guest speaker before writer's groups and at universities.

Steve's writing output increased dramatically when he emerged as one of the country's most in-demand writers of adventure paperback novels, averaging four books per year for ten years. His work on Don Pendleton's Mack Bolan series is regarded by fans as some of the best in that series. He also created the Mark Stone: MIA Hunter and Cody's Army series, written under the pseudonyms Jack Buchanan and Jim Case respectively.

Stephen Mertz lives in the American Southwest, and he is always at work on a new book.